P9-DDS-663

Fruitlands

Also by Gloria Whelan

ANGEL ON THE SQUARE

HOMELESS BIRD

THE INDIAN SCHOOL

MIRANDA'S LAST STAND

THE ISLAND TRILOGY:

ONCE ON THIS ISLAND

FAREWELL TO THE ISLAND

RETURN TO THE ISLAND

GLORIA WHELAN

Fruitlands

Louisa May Alcott Made Perfect

■ HARPERCOLLINS*PUBLISHERS*

Fruitlands

Copyright © 2002 by Gloria Whelan

All rights reserved.

No part of this book may be used or reproduced in any manner whatsoever without written permission except in the case of brief quotations embodied in critical articles and reviews. Printed in the United States of America. For information address HarperCollins Children's Books, a division of HarperCollins Publishers, 1350 Avenue of the Americas, New York, NY 10019.

www.harperchildrens.com

Library of Congress Cataloging-in-Publication Data
Whelan, Gloria.

   Fruitlands / Gloria Whelan.

     p. cm.

   Summary: Fictional diary entries recount the true-life efforts of Louisa May Alcott's family to establish a utopian community known as Fruitlands in Massachusetts in 1843.

   ISBN 0-06-623815-3 — ISBN 0-06-623816-1 (lib. bdg.)

   1. Alcott, Louisa May, 1832–1888—Family—Juvenile fiction.
[1. Alcott, Louisa May, 1832–1888—Family—Fiction.
2. Utopias—Fiction.   3. Family life—Massachusetts—Fiction.
4. Massachusetts—History—1775–1865—Fiction.   5. Diaries.]
I. Title.

PZ7.W5718 Fr   2002   2002001467
[Fic]—dc21   CIP
                                 AC

First Edition

Typography by Hilary Zarycky

1 2 3 4 5 6 7 8 9 10

To Alexandra and Michael

AUTHOR'S NOTE

In 1843, when Louisa May Alcott was ten years old, Louisa, her sisters Anna, twelve, Lizzie, seven, and two-year-old Abby May settled with their mother and father on a farm they called Fruitlands. It was the dream of Louisa's father to gather around him men and women who shared his vision of a more perfect world. Louisa's experiences at Fruitlands were both sad and funny.

From the time she first learned to write, Louisa kept a journal. It is believed that her father destroyed a part of her Fruitlands journal. Louisa herself, when she was older, destroyed many of her diaries. Only nine brief journal entries about her eight months at Fruitlands remain. I have imagined the diary that Louisa might have kept as well as a secret diary that told of her thoughts. This book is fiction, but it is based on real happenings. Fruitlands itself is now a wonderful museum where you may see, among many mementos of those days, the attic where Louisa and her sisters slept and a lock of Louisa's hair.

Fruitlands

—ᴟ—

JUNE 1, 1843

We are all going to be made perfect. This day we left Concord in the rain to travel by wagon the ten miles to our new home, which Father has named Fruitlands. The wagon was piled high with our possessions. Father drove the wagon. Mother was beside him holding two-year-old Abby May. Mr. Lane and Anna set us a good example by walking while I sat selfishly in the wagon with Lizzie. Mr. Lane's son, William, who is twelve, also rode in the wagon, though we had little to do with him.

The countryside around here is very pretty. Our new house is set on a hill. There is a stream and a wood nearby. In the distance I can just make out Mt. Monadnock stretched out like a sleeping giant. I feel much comforted by so fine a sight.

There is a snowfall of white syringa blossoms around the house. Their sweet scent, along with the perfume of the lilacs, pours in through the open windows to cheer us.

Our new home has a small dining room, a library for Mr. Lane's many books, and a large kitchen for Mother. Above are bedrooms. William is to have his own room. Anna, Lizzie, and I will share the attic. Abby May will be in Mother and Father's room. The other rooms are for Mr. Lane and the new members we hope to add to our family. The house was built before our Revolution. The floors tip this way and that, and the floorboards squeak and groan when you jump upon them, which Lizzie and I did.

Father and Mr. Lane are removing us from the imperfect world. By the fine example we all set at Fruitlands, we are to be a means of improving mankind. We will do nothing that might harm our brother animals. We will eat only fruit, vegetables, and grains. Because milk belongs to the cow and her calf, we will drink only water.

Father says we may eat those things that grow upright, aspiring to the air, such as apples, wheat, and cabbage. We are not to eat base things like potatoes and beets, which grow downward into the dirt.

When Father visited Mr. Lane in England, Mr. Lane was so impressed with Father's ideas that he and his son, William, left England to join us. It is Mr. Lane's generosity that is paying for all of this, but it is Father's vision that has led us to begin this new life. Father says that each man should live his own life, not as others live theirs. I pray that I can curb my temper and my laziness so that my behavior will be worthy of Father's high purpose.

I will put down a record of all that happens, for Father says that a journal is the way to come to know yourself, and it is only by knowing yourself that you are free to become yourself.

—⁓—

JUNE 2, 1843

This is to be my secret diary. Mother says our diaries ought to be a record of pure thoughts and good actions. She and Father often peek into our diaries to see that it is so. Yet Father tells us that we must be honest in our thoughts. I don't see how the two fit together. I am resolved to keep two diaries, one to share with Mother and Father, and this one which shall be my honest thoughts. In the first diary there will be Louy, who will try to be just what Mother and Father would wish. In the second diary there will be Louisa, just as she is.

I cried at leaving our dear little home in Concord yesterday and all of our friends, especially Mr. Emerson and my great friend, Mr. Thoreau. It was Mr. Emerson who gave Father the money for his trip to England, so Mr. Emerson takes a great interest in Father's plans. Before we left I overheard Mr. Emerson say about our scheme, "It may go well in the summer, but what of the winter?" His words sent a chill down my spine, for no one is smarter than Mr. Emerson. Even Mr. Emerson agrees to that.

Our journey was a miserable one. Mother held an umbrella over baby Abbie May, who didn't mind the trip but played at catching raindrops. It was raining so hard that we smelled like a wagonful of wet dogs. To make room for all of our possessions, Mr. Lane and Anna walked alongside the wagon. Mr. Lane is to teach us all how we are to improve ourselves. I watched him stride along behind the wagon, his head up, his chin out, proud of walking while others rode. He did not look like a man who thought he needed improvement.

Anna, who is twelve, two years older than I am, and much better than I, plodded along beside him. Toward the end, Anna's boots and skirts were all muddy, and her wet hair hung down like strands of seaweed. Giving me one of his disapproving looks, Father told Anna he was proud of her unselfishness in walking. I seem never to be able to please Father.

Because Father named our new place Fruitlands, I had hoped there would be an orchard, but there are only a few ancient apple trees. This is troubling, for fruit is to be the greater part of our diet. Still, a woods lies nearby and a gentle stream. Perhaps I will find an escape there from Mr. Lane's hard lessons.

I am not alone in my worries over our new life. Though she tried to hide them, there were tears in Mother's eyes as she saw all that needed doing to make our new home liveable.

Anna, Lizzie, and I sleep in the attic, which is dusty and dark and full of cobwebs and spiders. I helped Anna open the two small windows, for the attic was musty smelling as if it had been closed off for years. The ceiling is so low, we kept bumping our heads. When it grew dark, I made up a story for Anna and Lizzie about a fair maiden who was locked up in the attic because she refused to marry an evil old man. I said the creaking we heard was the maiden's ghost looking for a way to escape. Lizzie said we must leave the door open for the maiden, but I said the evil old man had put a spell on the attic. He set the spiders to weave magic webs so the maiden couldn't escape. If she tried, the cobwebs would wrap round her and smother her.

There was so much to do yesterday that none of the bedsteads were put up, so that we had to sleep on the floor. Though all my bones ached, I rejoiced in the thought of Mr. Lane stretched out on the hard boards. Lizzie would not sleep by herself but crept next to me, saying she had heard the maiden sigh. I tossed and turned. Anna slept very well, which is a sign of a clear conscience.

—⁓—

JUNE 3, 1843

We were up early to explore our new home. All I see is a large old house on a hill with acres of woods and meadow and, close by, the Still River. Father sees what the future will bring. He took Mother and me and my sisters outside and told us the name of the hill on which our house rests. The name is Wachusett, an Indian name.

Father is very tall with noble features and flowing locks. As he stood there telling us of his dream for Fruitlands, I was sure that others hearing of our way of life will be eager to join us. We shall build cottages for them on the hill. There are springs nearby. Father says the springs will be turned into fountains to cascade down the hill so that each cottage will have its own water.

He swept an arm over the meadow where cattle once grazed. "That is where we will grow our crops," he said. "Over there we will plant an orchard with pear, apple, cherry, and peach trees."

While Father spoke, all that he described was before my eyes, as real as if it were there. Mother and my sisters and I joined hands with Father. I am sure that this time Father's dream will come true.

—⁓—

JUNE 3, 1843

How I miss my dear little room in Concord. My back was sore from sleeping on the floor. There was nothing but apples and water for breakfast, and my stomach groans with hunger.

Abby May had a temper fit because she wasn't allowed milk, and Mother told her a story of a dear little calf who needed the mother cow's milk.

I try very hard to believe in Father's dreams as strongly as he does. I think him brave to keep dreaming, for he has had many bitter disappointments. I cannot forget how the school he started in Boston ended in failure. People did not appreciate his advanced method of instructing children. He believed in kindness and discussion instead of the ruler and learning by rote. For that he was criticized and the children taken out of his school. He lost all of his money. Though I was only four, I will never forget the sheriff knocking on the door of the school, carrying away the very desks and pictures on the wall. When the sheriff reached for my favorite picture, Flight into Egypt, *I ran at the sheriff, calling out, "Go away, bad man!"*

Father is surely an example for all of us. He does not dwell on his failures but tries again. Mother says this time he will be successful, for his dream is such a pure and good one.

Anna and Lizzie and I talked of Father's plans. Anna said, "If they could only hear Father as we did just now, I am sure the whole world would come to Fruitlands."

I said, "Mother wouldn't be able to cook for the whole world."

Lizzie said, "Father is like Moses, who led his people to the Promised Land." Perhaps we will find manna dished out on the meadows of Fruitlands.

This afternoon I looked about for a place to write my secret journal. I cannot write my secrets while others are watching, for these are private thoughts. It is too stuffy in the attic, so I searched outside. Some distance from the house I found a weeping willow tree. It stands close to the river, and its overhanging branches form a curtain. When I pushed the branches aside, there was a leafy tent I could crawl inside and be invisible to all. Even the small animals. While I am hiding away, making no sound, a cottontail rabbit sits just outside the tree branches grooming its fur and twitching its whiskers.

I have hidden in my leafy bower for a half hour. The breeze gently moves the trailing branches this way and that, so that first one part of land is visible and then another. It is as if pages in a book of pictures are being turned for me.

I know I ought to be helping Mother to air the bedding, but there is something in me that makes me want to hide away and just be by myself. When I am with my sisters, whom I love dearly, I have trouble remembering I am Louisa. Being with other people nudges me first one way and then another

11

until I hardly recognize myself. When I write my journal, putting down my thoughts, I find myself again.

Anna keeps a journal too, though I don't believe she keeps a secret one. I don't think she has any thoughts she needs to hide. Once I asked her, "Suppose you could climb into any page of your journal you liked and relive that page, would you want to?" "Oh, yes, any page at all," she said.

Too many of my pages list my faults, like the day I ran away from home when I was six, but here and there are records of perfect days I would like to live again. There is the day Mr. Thoreau let me walk with him right down the middle of a small stream, as much at home in the water as the ducks and muskrats.

—◊—

JUNE 4, 1843

Though it is a little crowded, we are fortunate that other fine people wish to join us in our efforts. Besides our own family and Mr. Lane and his son, William, we hope there will be several others who wish to live simply and close to nature. Mr. Lane says that each member of our community will be like a drop of fresh water falling into a cup until our thirst for a better life is satisfied. I am resolved to learn from all, and never again to be so rude as to laugh at Mr. Bower.

—⁓—

JUNE 4, 1843

What a strange lot we are! Joining us daily from his nearby farm is elderly Mr. Palmer. Mr. Palmer has a beard that reaches to his belt buckle. For a time men with beards were much looked down upon. Once four men set upon poor Mr. Palmer with the intention of cutting off his beard. He beat them badly. He was arrested and jailed for a year for refusing to pay a fine. At last he was told he might go. He refused to leave the jail, so they carried him out sitting on a chair. He is a stubborn man but a good farmer.

There is also Mr. Bower, who has a great love of nature. He will spend long minutes in the contemplation of a butterfly or a daisy but little time with a rake or a hoe. The strange thing about him is that he believes clothes are a hindrance to the growth of the spirit. Mother is very firm and says he must wear clothes when he is about, so he spends time shut up in his room letting his spirit grow. William looked through the keyhole and reported Mr. Bower was indeed in a state of nature!

William is thin with a washed-out look. He is quiet and well behaved when his father is by, but when he is with us he is more lively. I have warned Lizzie and Anna to have a care about saying in his hearing anything they would not wish to have Mr. Lane hear. I fear William carries tales.

—m—

JUNE 5, 1843

I am resolved to put aside my base hungers and eat only those things which uplift the soul. Today Mr. Lane explained how animals are our brothers. We are never to eat flesh or poor fish that have been caught with cruel hooks and snatched from the water. We are not to eat butter or rob hens of their eggs. I will do all that I can to curb my coarse appetites.

Mr. Lane has kindly drawn up patterns for our clothes. Mama has made them. They are not cotton, for that would be unfair to the slaves in the South who are forced to pick the cotton in the terrible heat. Father said the clothes must not be made of silk either, for silk comes from making the poor silkworms work long hours. Our garments are made of homespun brown linen and very plain. When our shoes wear out, Mr. Lane will tell us how to make shoes from canvas.

It will be a trial to me to think that I shall not be able to wear my lavender cotton muslin with sprigs of lilac all over and a ruffle at the hem, but I will try to keep an obedient heart.

—␣␣—

JUNE 5, 1843

Lizzie, Anna, and I nearly collapsed with laughter when we saw ourselves dressed in Mr. Lane's costumes. The men are in floppy trousers, long coats, and hats as big as platters. I think Mr. Lane must hate women, for it is the female clothes that are so hideous. We wear voluminous pantaloons, so large we might easily hide a cow in each leg. Over these monstrosities go long tunics. Little Abby May looks like a laundry bag tied in half, and poor Mother shed tears when she saw how she appeared. All these hateful garments are in coarse linen. They itch and are so stiff that when you sit down, they don't sit with you.

Mr. Wood Abram has joined us. He is a silent, glowering young man who has changed his name from Abram Wood, which is confusing, so I just call him Mr. Wood, for he is as silent as a tree. I asked him why, but for an answer he gave me only a dark look.

The men are busy in the forest cutting wood for the cookstove. They have planted some fruit trees, and today they began to plow. There was a great argument.

Mr. Palmer, his beard wagging with each word, said, "You can't plow without a team of oxen."

Mr. Lane shook his head. "We will not begin work by oppressing animals."

Father agreed. "Surely it is wrong to subjugate animals by hitching them to a yoke."

Mr. Bower did not give an opinion, for he was in his room growing his spirit.

When it came time to draw the plow, it was yoked to Mr. Lane. After a few hours his back hurt so he could not straighten up.

"It's against my principles," he told Mr. Palmer, "but

perhaps we will make this one exception. You may go to your farm and bring back your team of oxen."

Better the oxen's backs than Mr. Lane's! Mother, who was laboring over a hot stove, gave a great sigh and said, "The ox is not the only beast of burden at Fruitlands."

The men will plant clover and buckwheat to enrich the soil. They will not use manure to fertilize the fields.

Father says, "Such filth would enter our bodies through the crops we grew and would certainly poison us."

Can Father be right? Anna and I argued about it. Anna says Father would not say it if it weren't true. I said every farm I ever heard of used manure. Surely if what Father says is true, nearly everyone would be lying about dead. Neither Anna nor I would give in, so we ran about in the fields and pulled up grass and sucked the sweet part at the ends of the grass blades and made a daisy chain for Abby's golden curls.

—⁂—

JUNE 10, 1843

Father told us the story of a man who delighted not in accumulating money but in giving it to others. In secret he would put coins on the roadway for strangers

17

to find. His satisfaction came because he gave pleasure to others without calling attention to his unselfishness. I mean to take this lesson to heart.

Father gave us a length of rope for skipping. He says it is good exercise.

—◊—

JUNE 10, 1843

I have done an unselfish deed and have not put it in my journal to boast of to Mother and Father, but here in my secret journal. I was making lunch for Anna and Lizzie and myself. There were only a few wild strawberries left. Though I am hungry all the time, having a more substantial frame than Anna and Lizzie, who are more delicately made, I gave the strawberries to them, saying I preferred applesauce. In truth, I hate the applesauce because it's sour. Our store of maple sugar is dwindling, and Mother is not allowed to use white sugar. When you take the applesauce into your mouth, its sourness bites you.

Anna knew how I felt, and it would have been a kindness on her part if she had shared her berries with me. Then I would have done a good deed and received my share anyhow.

Another pilgrim has come to Fruitlands, Mr. Samuel Larnard. Mr. Larnard, who is no more than twenty, once lived for a whole year on crackers and another whole year on apples. He frowned at me when I asked for a second piece of bread. Abby May, who has a fierce appetite, doesn't mind his frowns, and today she reached onto his plate and snatched away a piece of his bread. Father scolded Abby May. Mother put her hand over her mouth so that no one should see her smile.

This afternoon I took Anna and Lizzie off into the woods with me and said we must pretend we were in the banqueting room of a great castle. We pulled up grasses and scattered them around for rushes. A flat stone was our table. I said the chipmunks and squirrels were our great dogs lolling about waiting for us to throw bones from the table. Everyone told what they wanted for the feast. Lizzie said she would have slices of bread with lots of butter, even if butter did come from a cow. I shocked Anna by saying I would have a huge platter of bacon and eggs. Anna said she would have a dish of green beans. I said the dogs wouldn't want any of her leavings. She said they would and that the dogs had green fur and ate only vegetables.

—m—

JUNE 21, 1843

Our day begins at five in the morning with a healthful cold bath at the stream. It is very refreshing. Our baths are followed by songs, exercise, and a nourishing breakfast of bread and applesauce. When I complained that the applesauce was sour, Father explained that we must do without white sugar. The white sugar that comes to this country from the West Indies is the product of slaves.

Then it is time for our lessons. Mr. Lane teaches us. Today we had a lesson on not eating meat. He explained that the slaughtering of animals brings out man's cruel nature. We had a little arithmetic and a fine discussion of self-sacrifice, which is Mr. Lane's favorite subject. Mr. Lane helped me to see that I am selfish, thinking little of others. I must be willing to do without so that my soul may be strengthened.

—〰—

JUNE 21, 1843

Our baths today were the funniest sight you can imagine. First the men bathed in the stream, and when they returned

I went with Mama and my sisters for our baths.

Lizzie asked, "Must I take a bath with frogs?"

Anna complained, "There are fish nibbling at my toes."

The morning was cold, and Mother just splashed the water on her face and hands and did not go into the river at all.

Yesterday Father gave in and concocted showers for us. A rough wooden frame was placed near the stream and covered with sheets. Anna, Lizzie, and I along with Mother, who held Abby May, stood inside. Father climbed up some wooden steps and poured pitchers of water over us. After a minnow landed on Lizzie's head, Father poured the rest of the water through a sieve. After she was soaped, Abby May was so slippery and squirmed so, Mother could hardly hold her.

Mr. Abraham Everett has come to live with us. He has soft brown eyes and long hair which curls at the ends. He is a fine addition, for he says little and works hard, unlike the others who much prefer talk to work. He has asked me to call him Abraham.

—⚉—

JUNE 24, 1843

Today is Lizzie's birthday. She is eight years old. Anna and I tiptoed out of the attic before Lizzie was awake to join Mother and William. It was just dawn and the sky was pink at the edges. The air was full of the smell of sweet clover. There was such a chorus of birdsong, I could not help joining in and whistled as loudly as any of the birds. We hung Lizzie's presents on a small pine tree. Even Abby May had a present. She had wrapped up a dozen raisins she had saved from her dinner the night before. My present was a pincushion I had fashioned from a bit of bright blue ribbon Mother gave me. I think it the prettiest thing on the tree.

After breakfast we led Lizzie out into the woods for her surprise. Abraham said he must stay and work and did not go with us. Anna made oak-leaf wreaths for everyone to wear so that we all looked like wood sprites, even Mr. Lane, who wore his wreath cocked on one side of his head. We sang, and Father read a noble poem he had composed. I am sure nowhere in the world were people so happy on this morning as we were.

—∾—

JUNE 24, 1843

I could not have been more surprised. Mr. Lane played his

fiddle in such a merry way, he did not seem at all like the sour man he is most of the time. Perhaps his fiddle is like my pen when I use it. Perhaps his finer nature shines forth in his music as I sincerely hope mine shines forth in my writing, though I am afraid that is not always true.

Lizzie was delighted with her presents and danced about with pleasure. Lizzie has the best nature of all of us. She is cheerful and never cross. Unlike Anna, she does not show off her goodness.

Mother, who is at her happiest when we are happy, sang in a loud voice. Father stood over us smiling, but I could see he was thinking on some lesson he could make of the celebration so that all our pleasure should not be wasted.

—⁓—

JUNE 30, 1843

We are like bees in a hive, all of us busy at our tasks. Lizzie, Anna, and I are up at daybreak to help Mother prepare breakfast. As we eat, Father improves our minds by reading a passage from some great work. This morning we heard the words of the Quaker William Penn, who said we wash, dress, and perfume our bodies but are careless of our souls. The body, he said, shall have three or four new suits a year but the soul must wear its old clothes.

With those words ringing in our ears, Anna, Lizzie, and I try to be cheerful in our duties. We clear the table and wash the dishes while Mother begins the laundry. Soon we are all at the scrub board, our arms in suds up to our elbows, while Mother boils the bed linens in the copper kettle to get them spotless. There is no finer sight than white sheets spread over green grass to bleach in the sun. It is like a field of snow in the midst of summer.

Afterward I scour the copper kettle with a teacupful of vinegar and a tablespoonful of salt to make it shine. I smell of vinegar all afternoon.

The men, even William, are in the fields. They have planted three acres of corn, two acres of potatoes, winter wheat, and much barley, which will be our principal food this winter. Apple and pear trees have been planted and mulberry trees as well. I imagine the fruit trees in the spring with their blossoms floating on a blue sky.

Mother and I and my sisters have set out our

kitchen garden. The only thing better than a tub full of suds is a handful of dirt.

—⚏—

JUNE 30, 1843

Abraham helped Mother wring out the sheets. With his long dark hair and great brown eyes and his silent ways, Abraham is mysterious. He is the only one of the men to lend Mother a hand. I think perhaps he is an exiled prince from some far kingdom.

When he thought no one was about, Mr. Palmer went into the kitchen and made bay rum to comb through his whiskers. I glimpsed the recipe, which called for oil of bay, oil of neroli, alcohol, and water.

I made a dreadful mistake today and caused trouble for Mother. "Father," I asked, "how is it we can use soap when it is made from tallow, which comes from the cow?" No sooner were the words out of my mouth then I saw the horrified look on Mother's face. At once I realized what I had done. As long as nothing was said, Mother might use the soap, but once it had been said out loud that soap required tallow from a cow, all was nearly lost. Luckily Father is first a philosopher and secondly a friend of cows, for he said, "It would be wasteful and discourteous to the cow to throw away the soap we had already purchased before we aspired to higher ideals."

Mother breathed a sigh of relief, for she had wisely taken with us a large supply of soap.

Father also gave in when it came time to plant vegetables, letting Mother put base, downward-growing potatoes, radishes, and turnips in along with the squash and beans and peas.

I go out each day to see what seeds have sprouted. I am heartily sick of bread and applesauce. When I look at the bare earth, I imagine fat pea pods and dangles of beans so that my mouth waters. The radishes have already begun to form. Yesterday when no one was looking, I pulled one and ate it, though it was no larger than a kernel of corn. Afterward I was ashamed of my gross appetite, but it is hard to work when you are famished. Even my stomach growls at its hunger.

When I complained to Mother, she gently chided me. "If our hearts are willing, Louy, dear, our stomachs will follow."

After that I cried and resolved not to complain.

When our work was finished and our lessons done, I went running up and down the hills. No matter how miserable I am, when I run down a hill, I run so fast my misery can't catch up with me.

—⟋⟍—

July 1, 1843

Each morning after our shower we have our singing lesson. Everyone joins in. I wish we might have our breakfast first. I am sure that if my stomach were full, I could sing with a louder voice.

This afternoon I picked a bouquet of field daisies and put them on the table for our supper. After our meals Mr. Lane leads us in an edifying discussion. Today he kindly noticed my daisies and took them as a subject for our talk.

"Louisa has put a vase of flowers on the table," he said. "Let us think whether the flowers are better plucked and placed in a vase or growing in the field."

Father: Can we not agree that the field is their natural place?

Anna: When they are growing in the field, they last longer than they do in a vase of water.

Lizzie: But we can't see them in the field. Here they are right before our eyes.

Father: Is it not better that we exercise our limbs

and go into the fields so that we may see the flowers as nature meant us to?

Me: I am very sorry I plucked the flowers. After this I'll leave the flowers where they belong.

I cried and was sorry. It is generous of Mr. Lane to take so much notice of my faults and so help me to improve.

—∿—

JULY 1, 1843

There is so little in the way of food on our table that I thought to put daisies there to keep our minds off of our empty plates. As a result so many words fell upon them, the poor flowers withered before our eyes, thus proving Anna's point. Anna always takes Father's side. Mother didn't say anything, but after dinner, when Lizzie picked some orange hawkweed and put them with my daisies, Mother smiled.

Mother does not often disagree with Father, but this evening was such a time. While the men were in the fields, a neighbor brought over a sack of hickory nuts. Had Father been there, he would have refused them, for they are neither fruit nor vegetable. When Mother put out a plate of the nuts this

*evening along with a nutcracker, Father looked stormy, but
Mother said we must have them until such a time as more vegetables ripen. "The girls are losing weight, Bronson," she said.*

*Mr. Lane saw that William was staring hungrily at the
nuts. His eyebrows met over his nose as they do when he is
about to make a pronouncement. In a firm voice he said,
"Self-denial is the road to eternal life."*

*Mother is the only one among us who is not afraid of Mr.
Lane. She said, "If we are to die of starvation, we will find
the road to eternal life soon enough."*

*At last Father gave in and we fell upon the nuts, even
William. Only Mr. Lane abstained. Never has anything
tasted so good. But even better than the taste of the nuts was
Mr. Lane's defeat at Mother's hands. I saw William steal an
admiring look at her.*

—◊—

JULY 2, 1843

This morning Mr. Lane and Father led all of us in a
discussion of poetry and how it is one of mankind's
most noble efforts. We discussed our favorite poems.
Father chose Mr. Emerson's poetry, and Mr. Lane chose

Milton's *Paradise Lost*. I chose Bryant's "To a Water-fowl," for it is all about a bird that travels on its solitary way. I am so fond of the line "Lone wandering, but not lost." I said I thought I was like that waterfowl. Father said I was too young to guide myself like a lone bird but must fly with the flock, following those who are wiser than I am.

I took a long walk this afternoon by myself. When I returned, I made hollyhock dolls for Abby May.

—∾—

JULY 2, 1843

Father was right! I need others to guide me. I started off like the waterfowl to take a solitary walk. I decided to explore the path to the little town of Still River. When I had gone a mile or so, I came to a farmhouse. It was painted a cheerful yellow and had orange lilies growing along its walk. There was a stone barn with a lovely cow with great brown eyes and long eyelashes. I think Father is right, for I don't see how you could eat such a pretty animal. While I was looking at the cow, a lady came out and inquired as to my name and where I lived. Though a smile crossed her face when I said, "Fruitlands," she was very friendly and asked me if I would like a glass of cold raspberry juice. I gladly accepted, for I am hungry all the time. I sat on her porch and drank the juice and ate a large piece of cake. When I exclaimed at how tasty the cake was, she wrote down the recipe.

Here are the terrible things I ate: butter and milk (from the poor cow), eggs (stolen from chickens who were fenced in), and white sugar (made by the work of slaves in the West Indies).

Thanking her, I hurried away. I buried the recipe under a stone. To punish myself I did not eat the wild blueberries Lizzie and Anna had picked. Mother looked surprised and I said I was not feeling well. After dinner I was hungry and I thought of how delicious the cake was, eating it once more in my mind. Does that mean I was bad all over again?

—⚊⚊—

JULY 5, 1843

I expressed a wish for a lamp so I could read at night, but Mr. Lane told us of the cruel way whales are harpooned to get the whale oil for a lamp. Father says we had better go to bed early and get up early, reading by the light of day. Mother begged for a lamp, and Mr.

31

Lane and Father finally agreed. No one else is to have one.

By the light of Mother's lamp, Father read us a story from the journal of the Quaker John Woolman. A man was traveling and, being a considerable distance from his home, planned to spend the night in the home of an acquaintance. But when he drew near to the man's home and observed the unhappy condition of the man's slaves, he lit a fire and spent the night in the woods.

The acquaintance inquired as to why the man had not stopped with him. In answer the man said, "I had intended to come to thy house, but seeing thy slaves at their work and observing the manner of their dress, I had no liking to come and partake with thee."

Mr. Lane then talked with us upon the subject that all men are equal. I was rude and impertinent, for I asked Mr. Lane if we are all equal, why should he always be the one to tell us what to do? Even Mother was angry with my rudeness. I cried and begged Mr. Lane's pardon.

—⟋⟍—

JULY 5, 1843

Today we had our first peas from the garden. Lizzie and I shucked them and I confess that as many went into our mouths as into the pot. I believe they are better raw than cooked. Certainly there is more crunch.

Mother is patient, seldom questioning the decisions made by Father and Mr. Lane. However, I believe winning the battle of the nuts gave her courage. When it grew dark, Mother lit a lamp. At once Mr. Lane said there should be no burning of lamp oil. "The cooking and cleaning and gardening take all my daylight hours," Mother said. "If I cannot have a lamp for my mending, the mending will not be done." Whereupon she put the basket away.

Father and Mr. Lane conferred, and it was agreed that Mother should have a lamp but that no one else should have one. However, we are like moths around a candle, seating ourselves by Mother's feet to catch a bit of light with which to read.

I don't know what made me say such a rude thing to Mr. Lane. I was truly sorry. When she heard me crying into my pillow, Lizzie crept over and put her arm around me. Anna asked, "Louy, why must you always say just what you think?"

"Should I say what I don't think?" I countered.

"You should say nothing at all," Anna said.

That is beyond my doing.

—⚏—

JULY 6, 1843

The men have traveled to Concord to talk with Mr. Emerson. William went with them. Mother said that after we finish our tasks we may have a holiday! Lizzie dusted, Anna polished the furniture, and I blacked the stove. Now Anna is writing a poem, and Lizzie is making dresses for her dolls. I am resolved to spend the afternoon in the woods looking closely at nature, as Henry Thoreau taught me to do. I have seen him get down on all fours to get a beetle's view of things. He thought nothing of sitting alongside of a woodchuck a half hour at a time so as to know the creature better. He even spoke to the woodchuck in the woodchuck's language.

This is what I observed. First, a woodpecker. The woodpecker was hard to see, for it kept circling the tree trunk to hide from me. The bird is as large as a crow.

Its feathers are red, white, and black with a ruff of feathers on its head like a crown. The holes that it makes are large and nearly square instead of round.

Next I ran after a squirrel, the better to see it. Not looking where I was going, I ran right into a hornets' nest but escaped with only one sting. I know it is a fault of mine to rush headlong into things. Father has often said so, and now I have the sting on my leg to prove him right.

Having heard that it was good for stings, I applied some Viper's bugloss to the sting to ease the pain. The purplish-blue flower with a red center is very pretty, but it has such an ugly name I feel sorry for it. When the sting still burned, I stuck my leg in the stream. There are trout in the stream so quick you are not sure you see them.

Orange jewelweed grows along the bank and red cardinal flower. The tresses of willows lean over the water like Anna and me when we wash our hair. I found a tiny bird's nest in an alder bush. It was made of the softest, greenest moss so that I would have been pleased to have been born and raised in it like the nestlings.

JULY 6, 1843

The truth is I did more than stick my foot in the stream. I hiked up my skirts and waded in it. All the while I was thinking of dear Henry Thoreau. On such a day as this, had we still been living in Concord, I would have been in his company. Though he is a man who prefers the companionship of a woodchuck to that of a human, he allowed me to come along with him on his walks, naming the flowers as we walked. He would give a low, secret whistle, and crows would come to him and feed from his hand. It was as natural for him to walk down the middle of a river as it was for him to walk along a path. He would declare, "I am in the same bathtub as the muskrat."

Anna and I went to Henry's school in Concord, but I learned more by following him along on his walks. He is not a handsome man; rather, with his long nose, some would consider him ugly. Yet his eyes are very fine and his manner so amusing, there is no one in whose company I would rather be.

Thinking of his walks in the river, I hiked up my skirts and waded in the stream, eating mouthfuls of watercress as I went. The current of the river made the sand slip out from under my toes. Bright-red cardinal flowers bloomed along the bank. A turtle pulled in its head and wouldn't look at me. A heron waded just ahead, its cruel beak ready to spear any poor frog that happened in its way.

I had meant to keep to the shallows and hold my pantaloons clear of the water, but there was so much to see, I forgot to take care. I had to lay my pantaloons and tunic in the sun to dry while I hid in the bushes.

It was the best day I have had since we came to Fruitlands. Mother tells me that I am a part of a glorious experiment, but I wish someone else had tried it all out before to see if living as we do would really work.

—◊◊◊—

JULY 8, 1843

We girls went with Mother to visit the Shakers who live nearby. Mother wishes to purchase a few yards of the fine linen they weave. The Shakers broke away from the Quaker church. All I know of them is that they dance and sing and shake away their sins.

There was no shaking when we visited their house, but only a quiet, polite welcome. The women wear poke bonnets and the men wide-brimmed hats. Mother whispered that she had never seen so spotless a house. There were no ornaments set about to prettify the rooms, only those things needful for everyday living. Yet with nothing fancy on which to feast your eyes, the simple well-made lines of the chairs and tables were pleasant. They have wooden pegs on the wall on which to hang their chairs. With all the chairs fastened to the wall, sweeping the room must be an easy task.

There are seed packets for sale and dried herbs to cure every kind of ailment. There were lovely-smelling packets of lemon balm, angelica, and lavender and bottles of rosewater.

Mother marveled over the cleverness of their bathtub. It is on the second floor, directly over the big wood stove in the kitchen. The tub is filled with water and the water left to warm from the heat of the stove. I will think of the arrangement this winter when we take our shower baths.

On one wall was hung the motto of the Quakers: "Hearts to Pray With; Hands to Work With." I mean to try to make it my own motto.

When we came home, Mother set us all to work so that we might follow the example of the Shakers' spotless home. Though it took all afternoon, everything shines to Mother's liking. Father says would not our time have been better spent in some effort to rub away the dust that has settled inside of our heads.

—⁓—

JULY 8, 1843

The Shakers were very kind to us, but I do not think they live as married men and women usually do. All the men live in one part of the house and all the women in another. Also, there was a ladder and a platform in the yard to aid the women in climbing onto a horse so that they would need no help from a man. It is against the Shaker rules for a woman or a man to touch one another. Is that not a strange rule? I asked Mother where Shaker babies would come from. She said the Shakers took in orphans.

Mother gave her shoes to the Shaker cobbler to have a new sole put on. It is to be a secret, for the sole must be leather. Mother dreads having to do her work in canvas shoes. For myself I keep my shoes from wearing out by going barefoot, but my feet won't stop growing, and now I have trouble squeezing into my shoes.

After the cleaning was done, I made up a game about the Shakers. William and I wore beards made from yarn and played the part of the men. Lizzie and Anna were the women and wore sunbonnets. We danced and whirled about and shook to get rid of our sins. It must not have worked, for I was soon in trouble. Father said he was much displeased at my game, for it was sinful to make fun of the beliefs of others.

I meant it in good fun, for I was truly impressed with the little community and thought their home very pleasant. It is a great weakness in me that I am not serious enough and make fun of everything. Yet I never mind when others make sport of me, and I like to join in the fun.

—⁓—

JULY 12, 1843

This morning Father repaired the house and the barn. He is as fine a carpenter as anyone. In the afternoon he left off his repairs and built a little hut in the woods of twisted branches and gnarled wood. It looks like elves live there. Father is so clever with his hands, he has often bartered his skills for food and shelter.

Mr. Hecker arrived today. We are pleased to have a new member of our family.

—☊—

JULY 12, 1843

Of all the men who are a part of our family I like Abraham best. He helps Mother with the laundry and in kneading the bread dough. I believe Mr. Lane looks down upon him for doing women's work, but Mother is grateful.

Abraham's is a sad story. He was once confined to an asylum by his greedy relatives who wanted to get at his property. It seems odd to me that after such an experience, he would believe that men could be made perfect. At least with his helping ways he is more perfect than many I could name.

Bugs have appeared on the potato plants. Mr. Hecker and Mr. Palmer would have us pick them off of the plants and drop them into a can of kerosene. Father and Mr. Lane say that is cruel. They say we must collect them and take them across the river. It takes twice as long to capture them and place them into a box so they can't escape. Mr. Hecker says it is foolishness. Father says Mr. Hecker does not understand our purpose at Fruitlands.

I doubt Mr. Hecker will remain. He doesn't get along with Father. The suggestions he made were turned aside. I heard him say Father thought too well of himself. Father, he said, could never pray, for he believed no one superior to himself. However, Mr. Hecker immediately went to work in the field. He left the bugs to us, but I am sure I saw him squish one between his thumb and finger.

—m—

JULY 14, 1843

Though it is summer we still have lessons. We meet each morning in the small dining room, where a bust of the Greek teacher Socrates looks down upon us with a cross expression on his face. There is also a globe of the world. William joins us, and Mr. Lane and Father are the teachers. Father says that children are born with a great deal of knowledge. The job of the teacher is not to impart knowledge but to arouse the conscience. This comes about by the questions which are put to us. "What is our idea of goodness?" "How do we know when we have done a bad thing?" "What is our task here on Earth?"

Sometimes Mr. Bower, Mr. Palmer, Mr. Wood, and Abraham join in our discussions, which become very lively. I am aware of how little I have to contribute to such talks. I am sure Father is right. Somewhere inside me I have the answers to his questions, but I am not very good at finding them. And I can't find the answers to long division at all.

—◊◊◊—

JULY 14, 1843

I do not see that I will ever be able to keep simple accounts, for no one but Mr. Lane seems to feel arithmetic of any value. Father never wishes to discuss numbers. When Mother brings them up to say we have no money, Father tells her he cannot be bothered with such things. Perhaps if Father knew a little more about sums, he would understand why we are so poor.

Mr. Lane has spent all of his money to pay for Fruitlands and to keep us fed and clothed. I have seen him sit by himself and go over the account books with a worried look. His money has been used up. Yet we still have urgent needs.

I can't help wondering how we will meet them. Perhaps Mr. Lane wishes to be sure that although our father knows nothing of numbers, his children will, for Mr. Lane takes time in our lessons for the doing of sums.

Lizzie is good-natured and listens patiently to all the questions that Father puts to us. Anna tries hard to give the correct answers, but sometimes when the questions are difficult she pleads a headache and slips away. I say what comes into my head and know at once it is a foolish answer. I wish I could learn to keep my silence.

After our lessons it is a pleasure to put on my sunbonnet and go out to weed the garden. With what vengeance I pull up the weeds! With what vigor I ply the hoe! I learn little during lessons, but the sitting still makes me a good laborer when at last I am freed.

—※—

JULY 16, 1843

Today we are busy in the house and in the fields, for Mr. Emerson is coming to visit Fruitlands. Just as Mr. Thoreau is my best friend, Mr. Emerson is a best friend to Mother and Father. He is very wise and has given us money for our experiment here. We are all anxious for his good opinion of Fruitlands.

—◊◊—

JULY 16, 1843

I have heard Mr. Lane fussing about money. William says his father has spent all he had on Fruitlands, and he doesn't have any more. It is the same old story. We are to be impoverished once more. Father thinks it is shameful to work for wages, and he will not do it. This fall Mother will have to write to our grandfather or our uncle to beg for money. She has done it so often, she would rather die than do it again. I know she does it only to put food in our mouths. It makes me feel bad, but I don't see how we are to stop eating. We have enough from the garden to get through the summer but not enough for the winter.

That is the reason we all worked so hard to make Fruitlands look attractive to Mr. Emerson. He believes in Father's dream, but he likes his roast mutton and beef and his puddings. He would not sit down happily to a dinner of beans and peas. He would rather help us with money than live with us.

When he arrived, Mr. Emerson greeted us with enthusiasm. He is a tall man, and so thin he would hardly make a shadow. Like Henry Thoreau he has a large hawklike nose. His blond hair falls over his forehead, and his keen blue eyes miss nothing.

His visit began with a trip through the house. He was much taken with the library and all of Mr. Lane's books. In the upstairs he asked, "Where do the girls sleep?" Father waved his hand in the direction of the attic stairway, saying we had "spacious quarters" there. In truth we cannot walk upright in most of the attic, and the heat in the summer nights is beyond anything. Also spiders remain.

It was the same in the fields. Mr. Lane referred to the small sticks of trees they have planted as "the orchard." Father, sweeping his hand in the direction of the fields, spoke of the "bounteous harvest" that would feed us in the fall. Though there is much barley planted, I don't believe there is enough wheat for many loaves of bread, and even if there were, where would we get the money to have it ground into flour at the mill? Still, I truly think Father believed all he said.

Father sees a different world from the one we see. His eyes are bigger and his mind is larger. He can put apples on a bare twig and fill an empty field with golden wheat. While I wonder how I can keep my temper, Father sees a whole

universe where everyone loves everyone else. I am very proud
of him when he talks to Mr. Emerson of how our accomplish-
ments at Fruitlands will help the world be better. I am glad I
am a part of Fruitlands. I am happy to take the rugs outside
and beat out the sand and dirt. I feel like I am cleaning up
the whole world.

Mr. Emerson has given money to us to help us survive.
I know everyone hopes that Mr. Emerson will tell others how
well we are doing here so that new members may join us and
bring funds with them. Yet I fear that will not happen, for
Mr. Emerson and Mr. Lane were like two dogs circling each
other, ready at a moment's notice to clamp their jaws on each
other's throats. Mr. Emerson confided to Mother that Mr. Lane
was a hopeless idealist. Mr. Lane whispered to Father that
Mr. Emerson would be nothing more than an observer at the
banquet of life.

—⟋⟍—

JULY 18, 1843

In the afternoon I was allowed to dust Mr. Lane's
books. There are nearly a thousand of them. Some are
in German, some in Latin and Greek. I read as I dust,

but there is no story to cheer you in any of them, only such thoughts as would make you hang your head and sigh a deep sigh. Here is one of the titles: *Synopsis Antiquitatum Hebraicarum.*

After dinner we had our usual post office.

—ɯ—

July 18, 1843

At any time during the day we may put our thoughts and questions on a scrap of paper and drop them into a little post office box. After supper Father reads out the scraps of paper. Here are today's scraps:

From Father: I have noticed that at breakfast there is not the spirit of cheerful friendship that we might wish. Let us all remember that we are here to make a brighter, happier world. We must start the day on the proper note, saying to ourselves the words of the great poet Milton:

> *Sweet is the breath of morn, her rising sweet,*
> *With charm of earliest birds.*

From Mr. Lane: Our dinner plates are overflowing. We must not allow the bounteous harvest from the garden to turn us all into gluttons. Greediness is always to be avoided.

The hungry man will always be more alert.

From Lizzie: I hope everyone will keep away from the side porch until the little mice nesting in Mother's vegetable basket are all grown.

From Mr. Bower: I see no reason why I was forced to go back to my room and put on clothes this morning. In this sweltering weather clothes are the greatest nonsense and interfere with our physical and spiritual health. It is a pity no one listens to me.

From Anna: I am resolved to be more useful and would be happy to take upon myself any tasks that need doing.

From Mr. Wood: Nothing, only a frown and the flash of his dark eyes.

From Mr. Palmer: Someone's got to start carrying water to the new fruit trees. They're drying up. The raspberry bushes need pruning. All that singing and talking around the breakfast table won't get the wheat in before the rain comes.

From William: I don't see why I always have to have my lessons with the girls, as I know more than they do.

From Mother: The girls worked very hard today to help me with the dusting. Louy dusted all the books, and there are a great many. Anna cleaned the potatoes for storage, and Lizzie polished the furniture with a fine polish which

Abraham made for me of linseed oil, beeswax, and turpentine. If I was a little cross at breakfast this morning, it is only that I was up most of the night trying to iron and mend the men's clothes so that they may do credit to Fruitlands when they go to New York this week. I would wish that all in that city should know of our brave efforts here to make a better world.

From Abraham: Got the south field plowed. Could have used some help.

From Mr. Larnard: I see no need for all this cooking of vegetables. Why not set out a pan of peas, beans, carrots, and onions, and we can eat them in their raw state as we pass by.

From me: I was much impressed with the seriousness of Mr. Lane's books. I think there would be nothing nicer than to write a book, especially one that everyone would want to read, not like the ones Mr. Lane has on his shelves.

Mother said I was rude, and Father said I was showing ignorance. I cried and apologized to Mr. Lane. I seem always to be apologizing to Mr. Lane.

—m—

JULY 24, 1843

Today we said good-bye to Mr. Hecker.

—⁓—

JULY 24, 1843

All was calamity and upheaval. This morning Mr. Hecker announced that he was leaving Fruitlands. We were all very sad and begged him to stay.

He said, "You do not have the Eternal here."

Mr. Lane asked, "What do you mean?"

Mr. Hecker said, "You think you can do everything without God's help." He scowled and added, "There are other things."

"What things?" Father asked.

"We are pledged to eat fruit, and there is no fruit here."

Father said, "Trees have been planted and the fruit will come."

"Not for many years," Mr. Hecker replied. "And to tell you the truth, Mr. Alcott, you are too high-handed."

Lizzie, Anna, and I gasped at such words. We had never heard Father criticized to his face and in such a rude manner. Mother glared at Mr. Hecker. Father grew red in the face. I believe there would have been angry words, but Mr. Hecker did not stay to hear them.

After he was gone Mr. Lane looked sad and shook his head. "He wanted more than we had to give him," he said.

Father was still very angry. "The man is a coward," he said in a stern voice.

In the evening I walked by the river to get away from Fruitlands, for all the angry words still seemed to be flying about the house like wasps.

It is true I am sometimes critical of Father, but I am sure that is wrong, and I cannot like anyone who finds fault with him.

Instead of increasing, our little family is growing smaller. Who will be next?

—⁓—

JULY 30, 1843

It seems the harder Father tries to make me good, the worse I become. This morning I made a list of all my faults so that I may improve. My faults are: selfishness, losing my temper, and acting without thinking first of the consequences. When I look at the dismal list, I feel bad and don't know where to start. Anna says I should start with losing my temper because I usually lose my temper with her. Lizzie says maybe I should list my good points as well.

I am beginning to think I have none, for this afternoon I disgraced myself and led my sisters to do that which they should not have done. I most humbly apologized to Mr. Lane.

Mr. Wood Abram left today.

—⚏—

JULY 30, 1843

I said it was all my fault, but it wasn't fair for William to carry tales to his father. I made up a play for Anna and Lizzie and me to perform. William asked to be in the play, but we sent him away sulking. We couldn't very well explain to him that I was taking the part of his father, Mr. Lane. In the play I called him Mr. Pain. Anna was Mother and Lizzie was me. When Lizzie tried to pick a flower, I called out in an angry voice, "No, no. That is forbidden!" When Anna pretended to spread butter on a piece of bread, again I cried out, "That is forbidden." And so it went until Mr. Pain was jumping up and down whenever Anna took a breath and screaming, "That is forbidden!" We were all laughing and having a merry time, Lizzie begging, "Oh please, Mr. Pain, can't I even take one little breath," and me as Mr. Pain saying, "That is forbidden.

There are tiny flies and fleas flying about in the air, and you might breathe one in and kill it."

I happened to look up, and there, with a storm cloud of anger on his face, was Mr. Lane and, with him, Father. Since we were hidden in the woods in a place no one but William knew, we guessed at once that William had given us away. Mr. Lane turned on his heel, but Father bore down upon us. I was roundly scolded for making fun of Mr. Lane.

Father said, "Mr. Lane, with great unselfishness, has made this excellent experiment possible. He seeks to raise us up to a higher level, while you descend to a lower level than I had thought possible. Worse, you take your sisters with you. How are we to go forward with this noble experiment? We are here to help one another climb the ladder of excellence, and you behave in such a fashion and drag us all down. I cannot tell you how distressed I am."

By now I was perfectly miserable and sobbing out that I was sorry.

Father said that I must apologize to Mr. Lane and that I must also choose my own punishment. Though I was very hungry, I said I would go without my supper.

With red eyes and still snuffling, I approached Mr. Lane and humbly begged his pardon.

"I accept the apology, for we must all forgive one another," he said, "but I must tell you, Louisa, I am most disappointed in you. I had hoped for something better."

Worse was to come. Everyone at the supper table saw that I had no plate before me, and all understood my humiliation. Everyone looked the other way, and I believe that I could have gotten though the meal had it not been for what Father did.

"Louisa has deeply saddened me today by her thoughtless actions," he said. "I feel that as her father, I must take responsibility for what she has done. Therefore I, too, will go without supper." With that, Father pushed his plate from him. I ran from the table to the attic, where I cried until the night darkened the windows. Mother tried to comfort me, but I would not be comforted. Anna wrote a little poem for me about not losing heart and trying to do better. Lizzie came with a piece of bread hidden in her pocket.

I resolved to be good after this, but first I planned to get even with William. I told Mother how angry I was with William for telling tales on me to his father. Mother said that if I had not done something of which I was ashamed, there would have been nothing for William to tell. She also said if I got to know William better, I wouldn't be so angry with him. She reminded me that William has no mother to go to

with his problems and receive wise counsel as I do. Later
Mother sent me a note urging me to ask Father's forgiveness.
She said Father loved me very much and would be so pleased.
I did as she said, though it was very hard. Afterward I felt
better.

Though he seldom said a word and we cringed under his
dark glances, we were sorry to see Mr. Wood leave. We have
lost two members of our little family, and winter is still far
away.

—⁊⁊—

AUGUST 3, 1843

I took care of Abby May all afternoon while Mother
and Anna changed the bed linen, washed it, and put it
back, for we have only one set for each of the beds.
Now that Abby May is three, she can take walks with
me. She follows me about just as I followed Henry
Thoreau, and I show her things just as he showed me.
We found a small garter snake the same color as the
grass. I held it and Abby petted it, saying, "Nice snake."
I made a bracelet for her of dandelion chains. We
caught tadpoles that already had their back feet. We ate

mulberries, and I played "Here We Go Round the Mulberry Bush" with her. There were mushrooms in the woods, and we made a table and chairs with them for elves. I taught her some lines in French about the bridge in Avignon. Abby is good-natured and smiles all the time. Everyone loves her, even William, who drew her a picture of a cat and a mouse having tea together.

In the evening Father and Mr. Lane and the rest of the men had their evening discussion. Anna, Lizzie, and I sat on the porch steps and read as long as it was light. Mother sewed and listened to the men talk.

—∿∿—

AUGUST 3, 1843

William came by while I was taking care of Abby May. I told him I thought it was mean of him to tell his father on me. He looked sheepish, which is easy for him to do because he has smallish eyes, hair that hangs down over his forehead, and a meek way about him. I only wish he had a bell around his neck like some sheep do. That way you could tell when he was nearby.

"I'm sorry you got in trouble," he said with such a mumble I could hardly understand him.

"If you're so sorry, why did you go to your father with tales in the first place?"

"Papa is paying for most everything here. I don't think it's fair that you should make fun of him. Papa gave up a good job in England to come here. We had to sell our house so there would be enough money for Fruitlands. Now we have no place to go back to. Your father has friends nearby to help him, but Papa doesn't have anyone. Anyhow, Papa said I was right to tell him and I must tell him every time I see something like that." He looked even more sheepish than usual. "Papa said I was a good boy to go to him."

I was very cross with William. "If you mean to keep telling on us, I'd just as soon you stayed away."

William hung his head and began to walk away. I thought of what Mother had said about his having no one to confide in. I called him back. "It's all right to stay now. I'm not doing anything your father would disapprove of except maybe that I'm having fun with Abby May. He doesn't like people to amuse themselves."

"That's just the kind of thing you shouldn't say about Papa," William said.

"It's true your father doesn't seem to have a lot of fun."

William sighed. "I know." His shoulders sagged as if he were carrying a heavy burden. How much he reminded me of Christian in John Bunyan's The Pilgrim's Progress. Christian had to make his journey to the Celestial City carrying a heavy burden on his back. He lived in the City of Destruction and was condemned to death and judgment. Surely that is what it would be like to have as a father Mr. Lane, who is quick to judge and condemn people. In a way I can sympathize with William. William wants his father to think him a good boy, and I wish my father would approve of me instead of always pointing out my faults. But I wouldn't tell on anyone just so Father would say I was good.

"Why don't you stay and help me amuse Abby May?" I asked.

William smiled. "I could get my notebook and draw her a picture," he offered.

When Abby May giggled at his picture of a cat with long whiskers and a mouse with a curly tail, William actually smiled.

In the evening Anna and Lizzie and I played cards while the men talked and Mother sewed. The men never think to ask Mother's opinion.

Worse, they make schedules for Mother as to what she should be doing each hour of the day, but they do not consult her wishes. If she raises a question, Mr. Lane's eyebrow goes up and he says they ought not to be interrupted. If she asks the question anyhow, he takes out his pocket watch and consults it while she is talking. Mother must cook and sew and do the laundry for the men, but the men will not allow her to speak her mind. Surely that is not right.

Tonight Mother lost her temper, which she almost never does. She told the men, "I have a mind and a soul just as the rest of you do."

After that there was a long silence until Mr. Lane said, "I am sure that you do. If you listen quietly to these discussions of ours, both your mind and your soul are sure to grow, at which time you will be welcome to join our discussions."

I could see that Mother was trying hard to get her temper under control, and she did. If it were me, when I laundered Mr. Lane's trousers I would put so much starch in them that he would not be able to sit down. I would put sand in his bed when I made it. When I cooked for him I would leave the little worms in his cabbage.

—w—

AUGUST 8, 1843

A woman, Ann Page, came to Fruitlands today to see what we are doing here. She is rather old and a little fat and had too much to say. Mother and the men were busy showing her about, so Anna, Lizzie, and I were given leave to do as we pleased until she left. I wrote a story about a fairy kingdom, and we went out into the woods and acted it.

When we came back, Mother told us Miss Page might come and stay with us. She would help Mother and would give us piano lessons.

—⁓—

AUGUST 8, 1843

In my play Anna was the queen of the fairies, Lizzie was the good fairy, and I was the bad fairy. I got to cast evil spells and turned everyone into toads and lizards. Lizzie turned them back. We made dresses from Mother's old petticoats and wings from paper. We pinned the wings onto our dresses and flew by jumping off a tree stump.

Today Lizzie asked me why I'm always the villain and

the bad person when we act out our plays. I think it's because that's how I feel. Anna is Father's favorite. First of all she takes her problems to Father and asks for his advice. The trouble is her problems are all such little ones because she is so good. I have lots of faults and some of them are not so small. Anyhow, Father points out my faults without my ever mentioning them to him. Anna doesn't mind being punished for her faults. When I am punished I only become angrier, and that makes Father sad.

There is something else as well. Anna is blond and light-complected like Father. But I have dark hair and also I am dark-complected like Mother. Father believes that the lighter-complected you are, the higher up you are on the spiritual ladder. I think that is a cruel idea and wrong, for no one could be better than Mother. She thinks of everyone but herself, whereas Father hardly thinks of anyone but Father.

After supper I went out and watched the hills turn purple and the nighthawks drop. When other birds are on their nests, the nighthawks are still flying about. They fly up into the twilight sky and then plunge down as if they had been dropped from the heavens. Just before they reach the ground, they swoop upward. I think I am like the nighthawks. I have moods and a bad temper and I'm selfish, but I never *quite fall onto the ground. I catch myself, or Mother catches me, and I rise.*

—∿—

AUGUST 10, 1843

Each morning after we have our breakfast and our showers, we all sing together. This is my favorite time of day. Mr. Palmer's long beard goes up and down with the words. Mr. Lane has a fine voice, and Father sings with enthusiasm. William, Samuel Larnard, and Abraham join in. Mother's voice is rich and my sisters' voices sweet. Miss Page does not exert herself to sing. We can even hear Mr. Bower humming along with us in his room. All the songs we sing are uplifting. After the singing we go to our labors with light hearts.

—∿—

AUGUST 10, 1843

I wish that we might preserve the friendly lighthearted spirit of our singing all day. After the songs, our problems and disagreements return. I do not see how we are ever to be made perfect.

63

Here is what happened only an hour after our songs.

Mr. Palmer to Mr. Lane: You ought to be in the field hoeing the corn. The weeds are nearly as high as the cornstalks.

Mr. Lane: We are engaged in a serious discussion as to how work in the fields might be made more edifying. Might we not read aloud from a philosopher so that pure thoughts would accompany the work?

William (who does not like to work): I could be the one to read.

Father: What if we abandon the barley and wheat and the corn altogether and live upon the fruit from the orchard? The orchard requires little in the way of labor. We would therefore have more opportunity for discussion.

Abraham (putting down his hoe and wiping the sweat from his brow): It will be ten years before those trees produce enough fruit to satisfy our hunger.

For once his soft brown eyes were flashing.

Mr. Larnard: That is no matter. If I lived for a year on nothing but crackers, I do not see why we might not all do the same.

Of course with all the talk no work gets done.

Mother was inside and took no part in the discussion. She said to Miss Page, "Ann, I have all I can do to put up the raspberries. You might help out by sweeping the floors."

Miss Page replied, "You know the dust from sweeping settles in my nose and makes me sneeze. I have found a most interesting book in the library, Sacred Writings of the Ancient Persian Prophets. *I believe I will just take it outside under the trees and read a bit. You should do the same, for our purpose is to expand our minds. I do believe that you work too hard."*

Under her breath Mother said, "I work that we may not starve, especially those of us with a large appetite."

Miss Page is always the first at the table and takes the largest helpings.

Anna and I looked at the broom, each of us waiting for the other. Lizzie took it up and began to sweep. The broom was too big for her and I finally took it, but I was cross with Anna for leaving it to me to do.

Perhaps we should sing all day!

—⚊—

August 12, 1843

We spent the afternoon carrying water from the spring to Mother's kitchen garden. We have had no rain for a week. The cabbage is bolting, and the beans are freckled with brown spots. In the field the ears of corn we pick are wormy with borers. We put the borers in a jar and walked them to the other side of the river to join the potato bugs. We cooled off as we waded across the stream. Afterward I wrote a story about how the opposite side of the river was full of bugs waiting for a log to float by so all the bugs could make their way back to us.

It has been hot all week. The attic is so stuffy at night that Lizzie and I sleep under the window, and still it feels like we are in a glass bottle with the stopper in. Even the spiders that live in the attic are too warm to spin proper webs. I made friends with one of the spiders and leave his web alone. Tonight there were two small flies caught in the web. I let the flies escape, but what will the spider have to eat now? If the animals and insects did not eat one another, they would starve. On my scrap of paper today I asked if it would it be possible to have a kind of Fruitlands for animals and insects where they were more kindly to one another?

Father scolded me, saying I was making fun of our noble project. I cried and apologized.

Anna now has her very own room.

—⚍—

AUGUST 12, 1843

Father has taught us to use our heads and reason out every-thing, so I have reasoned out why Anna should have her own room. Here are the reasons. 1. She is older than I. 2. She is bigger than I am by an inch and therefore needs more room. 3. She is better behaved and more thoughtful of others and ought to be rewarded. 4. Father thinks her a better person than I am.

Setting down the reasons does not make me feel any better. I would have given anything to have my own room where I could think my own thoughts and scribble away whenever I wished. Reasons are all very well, but there are ever so many inches between my head and my heart.

—⚍—

AUGUST 14, 1843

This morning at the breakfast table Father asked, "What is the purpose of imagination?"

Anna said, "To reach for things more beautiful than those we see in the world."

I said, "To amuse ourselves when we are bored."

Father said Anna's answer showed more spiritual growth than mine.

William and I picked the wild mint that grows by the river. We crushed it and let it soak in water to make a refreshing drink. The tadpoles have their front feet now. The jewelweed that grows along the river's edge has gone to seed. When you touch the plant, the seeds jump out at you. I wish Henry Thoreau were here so I could show him.

Mother is teaching us how to knit. We will be able to make our own wool stockings against the winter.

Today Samuel Larnard left. Also there was trouble with Mr. Bower.

—∿—

Because he does not believe in clothes, Mr. Bower keeps to himself in his room during the day. At night he dons a long, loose white garment that is very like a nightgown and wanders about so that looking out the window you think you see a ghost. Last night he wore no garment at all but went wandering down the path in a state of nature. A neighbor saw him and chased him with a broom through a blackberry patch. Today he is sulking in his room, much wounded with scratches. Mr. Lane is afraid Mr. Bower's behavior will make people believe Fruitlands a strange place.

I do believe that even Mr. Lane's strict rule was not strict enough for Sam Larnard. It was Mr. Larnard's greatest pleasure to do without. We all stood at the door to see him off and waved him on his way. I believe as he got ready to leave, he began to regret his going, but he is a stubborn man and would not turn back. As he left he clasped Mother's hand and held it tenderly, a gentleness I would not have expected in so rough a nature. Father is troubled because we have lost three people now and there are no new prospects.

I felt downhearted and asked Mother what would happen if Fruitlands was a failure.

"Whether we succeed, or whether we fail, Louy, does not matter," Mother said. *"It is the attempt that is important. Who can fault us for aspiring to so noble a dream?"*

—◊—

AUGUST 16, 1843

William, Lizzie, Anna, and I found a patch of wild grapes. They were only a little sour. We made wreaths of the vines and togas from sheets and played at being Romans. When Father saw us he was much amused and made us sit down and discuss whether the Romans or the Greeks had the greater civilization. With the sheets wrapped around us and the vines on our heads it was very hot. We all cooled off in the river, Father as well. While in the river Father asked us to consider how the settlement of America has followed the course of rivers. We stood in the river and talked of geography until our toes were wrinkled and numb.

Miss Page left Fruitlands this evening.

—◊—

AUGUST 16, 1843

I know I should be sorry that Miss Page is gone, but I'm not. She scolded me for not singing in tune. She never did her share of work but sat and watched Mother and the rest of us labor away, never lifting a finger to help us.

She was expelled from Fruitlands for her sin as Adam and Eve were sent from the Garden of Eden. It happened in this fashion. Miss Page had visited a nearby farm. There she was offered some fish and she ate it! When Mr. Lane and Father accused her, she said she ate only a small bit of the tail. Mr. Lane said even so, all the fish had to be killed that she might have the tail. Though she sobbed most terribly, she was ordered to leave. I believe that Mother could have saved her, but Mother had grown tired of waiting upon her.

Along with my relief that she is going I have a terrible worry. What if it were discovered that I had eaten a piece of cake? Would I be sent from Fruitlands, never to see my mother and father and sisters again? The worry kept me awake all night. I listened to the screech owl and stood at the window looking out. There was a full moon, and I watched the bats dive for mosquitoes. I imagined myself cast out and living in

a woods with nothing but owls and bats for company and was
very sorry for myself, which made me feel better.

—⚍—

AUGUST 18, 1843

Mr. Parker Pillsbury came from Boston to tell us of the fight against slavery. The people of Boston have taken up the cause. Articles appear in all the papers. Even poets like Mr. Whittier are speaking out. I remember Henry Thoreau saying that it is wrong to pay taxes to a government that does nothing to end slavery.

People are learning of the miserable conditions under which the slaves live and how they are bought and sold like cattle and their families broken up. The merchants and cotton exporters who owe their living to slavery are the ones supporting its cruelty.

Mr. Pillsbury says the battle has just begun. He told us of an abolitionist who went about preaching against slavery. One day he received a package from the South. When he opened the package, he found a dried ear and a length of rope. The ear had been severed from a slave who attempted to escape. The length of rope was meant for the abolitionist if he ever attempted to go to the South.

Slaves who have been helped to escape are to be found on any Boston street. Many of the homes in Concord have a special room where escaped slaves are hidden. Now there is talk that a fugitive slave law might be passed. Such a law would punish those who help slaves to freedom. Mr. Pillsbury says one day there will be fighting in our country between those who support slavery and those who wish to end it. I would gladly fight in such a war. But what of the Quakers, who are against slavery but are opposed to all fighting, even for so noble a cause?

Tonight Abraham Everett left.

—✺—

AUGUST 18, 1843

I wrote a play about slaves and masters. My sisters and I were the slaves. William would agree to be the cruel master only if he could also be the one to free the slaves. After we were freed, we ran into the woods and hid and would not come out until Mother called us for supper.

After supper Abraham went up to his room and came down with all his things. He has been quiet these last days, spending more time by himself. I believe Mr. Pillsbury's talk today about slavery set him to thinking. While having Mr. Lane and Father over him is not slavery, still I believe he grew tired of being told what to do. After having been shut up in an asylum by his relatives, I think his need for freedom is very deep. My sisters and I cried when he left, and so did Mother. He has been the only one to help her. I have heard her call him "son."

No one is left now but Mr. Palmer, who is living at his farm and comes here each day, and Mr. Bower, whom you can't really count. How will we manage with so small a community?

—◊◊—

AUGUST 20, 1843

A needy family appeared at our door, a father and mother and two girls near the age of Anna and me. Their house has burned down and they have no food or clothes. Mother was much moved and gave them a basketful of vegetables from the garden, dishes, Father's trousers, Anna's blue dress, and my lavender cotton muslin with lilac sprigs and a ruffle at the hem. The girls looked very pleased and snatched at the dresses in a way I thought ill-bred. I was sad to see my dress disappear down the lane on the arm of one of the girls. I know we no longer wear the dresses, but sometimes I took my dress out and looked at it. Lizzie ran after the girls to give them one of her dolls.

I had the care of Abby May this afternoon. She is good-natured as long as she gets her way. So she is usually good-natured, for it is hard to deny her anything. She is so comely, with large blue eyes and golden curls.

We found a praying mantis sitting on a twig. It looked so much like a stick, you could hardly tell it from the twig. With its sharp elbows and knees it looked like Ichabod Crane in "The Legend of Sleepy Hollow."

In an alder bush along the river I showed Abby May a sparrow's nest. It was made of grass and moss all cleverly woven together and lined with feathers. In the nest were three small greenish-blue eggs and one large white egg speckled all over with freckles of brown.

We let a beetle, green as an emerald, crawl up and

down our arms until it got tired of the pastime and scampered away.

—⁓—

AUGUST 20, 1843

Today Father measured us. I have grown an inch, Anna an inch and a half, and Lizzie nearly two inches. It was hard to make Abby May stand still, but Father says she has grown nearly two and a half inches. He keeps a notebook with all of our measurements. He says that our soul grows just as our bodies do and that he marks the soul's progress down as well. I am sure my soul did not grow much today, for I was unhappy that Mother gave away my dress. I know that was selfish, but as long as I had the dress, I could believe I would not have to spend the rest of my life in coarse brown linen.

It is frightening to me to think my soul is looked at, even by Father. It is as if my soul were not my own but something to be handled and turned this way and that.

It is this habit of always examining all we say and do that makes me most unhappy. Here is an example from a conversation that took place this evening.

Louisa (with pride): I took Abby May out for a walk this

afternoon and showed her pretty things in nature.

Mr. Lane: What did you show her?

Louisa (still showing off): A praying mantis.

Mr. Lane: The praying mantis is a most unusual insect. The female of the species bites the head off the male.

Louisa: Ugh!

Mr. Lane: What else did you see?

Louisa: We saw a nest with three greenish-blue eggs and one large speckled white egg. I thought that very curious.

Mr. Lane: Do you know who put the large white egg there?

Louisa cautiously shakes her head.

Mr. Lane: A cowbird lays its egg in the nest of a smaller bird and then flies off, leaving the small bird to hatch the egg and feed the young cowbird. The cowbird's egg will hatch first. The young cowbird will eat so much that the young of the smaller birds may perish. What else did you see?

I was almost afraid to mention the beetle for fear Mr. Lane would make the beetle unpleasant too, but the beetle was so small I did not see how that was to be done.

Louisa: We saw a shiny green beetle with some red on it and a horn in the middle of its head.

Mr. Lane: That was a dung beetle. It lives in the filth of

a manure pile, forming a bit of the manure into a ball, which it then buries, later laying its eggs there. What lesson do you draw from my comments, Louisa?

Louisa: Not to tell what I have seen.

Father was cross with my answer. He said that I was impudent and that Mr. Lane was trying to point out that nature is neither pretty nor ugly, but always interesting.

I was glad Abby May was already asleep and did not have to have her afternoon walk spoiled as I did. There do not seem to be as many pleasant days as there were when we first came to Fruitlands.

AUGUST 23, 1843

Every one of us was on his knees yesterday, as if we were all in church, but we were digging potatoes and not praying. My knees are sore, and I can't get all the dirt from my fingernails.

Today we were upright, picking the last of the blackberries. I am sad that there won't be any more berries to pick until next June. Picking wild berries is my favorite thing. I like it because Mother puts on her sunbonnet and goes out into the woods with me and my sisters. Sometimes, as we did today, we pack a lunch and spend the whole day filling our pails. We sang songs as we picked and recited our favorite poems. Even Abby May picked some blackberries and ended up with her mouth and fingers all purple. I would like to live in the woods like a dryad, sleeping under the sun and moon, wearing flowers in my hair, climbing trees, and living upon wild berries.

—⁓—

AUGUST 23, 1843

We are more happy when we are away from Mr. Lane. Out in the woods I don't feel his critical eye on me. I am sure he is a very good man, but he is not a pleasant man. The only time I see him smile is when he plays his violin and sings along with it. Music makes him nicer than people do. The difference between him and Father is that Mr. Lane thinks you cannot have happiness unless you spend a lot of time being miserable. Father wishes us to be happy all the time.

We ate the last of the peas yesterday and the beans are dwindling. We still have cabbages and squash and pumpkins, so I guess we will have enough to eat for a while. Father says we can depend on the barley crop to see us through the winter.

Father and Mr. Lane leave tomorrow for New York City to try to interest more people in joining us.

Mother was happier in the woods today than she has been for a long time. She has to work so hard to cook and clean and sew for all of us. She seldom complains, but today on the way home from picking berries she sighed and said she wished she could make a blackberry pie. You cannot make a pie without lard, and lard comes from pigs. So no pie.

I am too old to play with dolls myself, but I helped Lizzie make new clothes for her dolls. She begged me to play at a tea party for the dolls, which I did. We made dandelion tea. I don't see why we have to be just one age all the time. It would be nice if we could be older sometimes and do just as we liked and then younger and still play with dolls.

—⁓—

SEPTEMBER 3, 1843

William and my sisters and I shucked corn all morning until we were covered head to toe with the sticky corn silk. Afterward we had a game of hide-and-seek among the cornstalks. We were hot from the running and sat on a log with our feet dangling in the river. William told us about England. We asked him if he missed living there. He said in England he had no family but his father. Now, at Fruitlands, we are all his family. I said he could be our brother forever.

In the afternoon we dried herbs: peppermint, rosemary, tansy, parsley, savory, and lavender. My hands smelled so lovely I didn't wash them for supper.

— ∿ —

SEPTEMBER 3, 1843

I was good almost all of today. It is easier to be good if you are busy.

Tonight Father told us how when he was a young man, unable to find work as a teacher, he became a peddler. He sold buttons and thimbles, shaving brushes, combs, scissors, and sewing threads. For five years he traveled all over the South, sleeping in slave quarters and nearly drowning in the Dismal Swamp of Virginia. He entered thousands of homes. Sometimes he was given a cold glass of water. Sometimes the dogs were set upon him. As Father told his story, I thought what a hard life he has had. Still, he is always in good spirits and full of hope. I try to be hopeful as well, but we seem to want for everything. When once a friend asked Mother if our poverty was not difficult for her, she said Father's tatters were the rags of righteousness. I thought that very beautiful. I mean to work harder and be more cheerful.

—ɯ—

SEPTEMBER 6, 1843

Yesterday all the men left the farm, Mr. Palmer and Mr. Bower to Boston and Father and Mr. Lane to New York. Father and Mr. Lane had no money for their travel, but they said they would board the boat in Boston and offer to give a lecture to the passengers in exchange for their passage. Mother had hoped they would change into their suits, but they said it was well that the rest of the world should see them in their linen tunics and trousers, the better to understand their purpose. William went with them.

Just at dark we had a very bad thunderstorm. Before the storm Mother and my sisters and I got in the barley harvest.

—⟋⟍—

Yesterday, before everyone left, Mother asked Father, "Bronson, shouldn't the barley be brought into the barn before you go?"

"The barley can wait until we return, my dear. What is of foremost importance now is to bring new people into our little experiment. We must spread the happy word. The barley is all cut, and we will only be gone a few days."

"But if it should rain?" Mother asked.

Mr. Lane looked up into the sky and said, "There will be no rain." I do think Mr. Lane believes he can make the rain come or go as he pleases.

Father said, "We must do our duty and trust to Providence."

The sun shone all day yesterday, and Mother said after we weeded the carrots and cabbage we might have a holiday. I made up a play about an enchanted island like Shakespeare's The Tempest. *We made a boat out of an old wooden box and shipwrecked it on the bank of the river. Anna was Prospero and the Prince, Lizzie was Miranda, and I was Caliban and looked as ugly and frightening as I could. Abby May, with her fairy looks, made a fine Ariel and took great delight in pinching me and making me fetch and carry.*

In the evening we all took our dinner outside and had a picnic.

This morning the sun disappeared, and all across the sky gray clouds were bumping into one another. The sun shone behind the clouds and lit their edges, so at first they were very pretty. In the afternoon the clouds turned black. Swords of lightning were thrust out of the sky followed by rumbling thunder. Mother ran in and out of the house, looking first at the sky and then at the barley lying upon the ground.

"If the rain falls on the barley it will rot, and we've no other crop to depend upon for food this winter," she said. She turned to us. "Girls, bring every basket in the house here. And quickly."

Lizzie, Anna, and I ran from room to room tumbling papers and firewood and sewing out of baskets, snatching them up and running with them to Mother. Even Abby May dragged a basket to the porch.

Handing the baskets out, Mother led us into the field. "We must be as quick as we can, girls. The barley is all that lies between us and starvation this winter." We flew up and down the rows gathering the sheaves of barley, piling them into our baskets, and running with them to the granary. Back and forth we ran, unmindful of the flashing and roaring over our heads. We bumped into one another, we tripped, we fell, the sheaves scratched our hands, and the barley got in our hair and down the necks of our dresses and itched. By the time the first drops of rain fell, we had saved a good part of the crop.

Mother hugged us all and told us our efforts had saved us from starving. I am not very fond of barley, but I am even less fond of starving, so I took satisfaction in our afternoon's work. I said, "Father told us Providence would provide."

Mother smiled at us. "Luckily, He had five helpers."

—⚹—

SEPTEMBER 14, 1843

We have had three days of rain, so I have been reading. There is nothing I like so well as to curl up in the attic with a book while the rain dances upon the roof and slides down the window. I will put down some of my favorite books. The first is *The Pilgrim's Progress*. I think the burden I carry of selfishness and thinking only of myself is very like the burden Christian carries on his journey past the Hill of Difficulty and the Valley of

Humiliation to the Celestial City. The next is *The Vicar of Wakefield*. Everyone in the book has faults as I have, but in spite of the fact that Dr. Primrose loses all of his money and is thrown into prison, it has a happy ending. Maybe I will, too.

—◊◊—

SEPTEMBER 14, 1843

Father says that we must read to find characters whom we wish to imitate. Though Christian and Dr. Primrose are such characters, I must confess that I like villains just as well. It really makes you want to turn the pages when you are hoping that something bad will finally happen to evil people.

Today on my paper scrap I wrote, "If sharing all we have with one another is so important, shouldn't Anna be made to let me have her room to myself sometimes?"

Father said I should be thinking of what I could share with others and not what I wished others to share with me. I let Anna wear my best blue ribbon around her hair.

—◊◊—

SEPTEMBER 28, 1843

Now that our berries and most of our vegetables are gone, we were happy to receive several barrels of apples. Mother wishes to get more maple sugar so that she can begin to make applesauce again, but Mr. Lane says that self-denial is the road to a spiritual life. He insists we eat our applesauce unsweetened. Mother said there must be more to life than doing without everything that might give one a little pleasure. A compromise was agreed upon. Mother is to use just a very little maple sugar.

—⚏—

SEPTEMBER 28, 1843

Everyone was cross tonight because of the applesauce discussion. Even Mother was cross. She says we are too much in one another's pockets. We see the same faces at all our meals and hear the same complaints. Mother must keep house for everyone, yet she has little say in decisions. I saw today that she meant for once to have her way. Since she is the one to measure the maple sugar, we can be sure the applesauce will be sweet.

When I was outside this morning, I noticed how still it was. There is no birdsong in the trees. Just like our five departed friends, the birds have all flown away from Fruitlands. The wild asters are gone, and the bracken turned brown overnight with the first frost. A shriveled blackberry dangles like a single earring. A few red leaves show on the maple trees, and the sun goes down early. We all gather around Mother's lamp in the evening now to read our books. It is cozy with a fire in the fireplace to keep us warm, but we can't take the warmth of the fire to the attic with us. The window rattles, and the wind blows through the cracks in the walls and the roof. What will it be like in the winter?

—\\\\\\—

OCTOBER 10, 1843

From our hillside we look out to see the trees all around us catch fire with autumn colors. Lizzie and I walked in the woods seeking the prettiest leaf. We could not choose, for one leaf was brighter than the last. We pressed some of the showiest leaves in books, but in a few days their colors will have faded. Though we work hard to make our little family a perfect one, all our months of sacrifice and work are not so fine as the maple tree beside the back porch. And we had nothing to do with that.

Mother sent us to gather butternuts. She said the Indians boiled them to obtain a kind of oil. She means to try to boil some herself. Now that the leaves are beginning to drop, it is easier to discover the butternut trees. We gathered the nuts until our hands were stained brown so that we stopped picking for a while and played at being Indians. There were once thousands and thousands of Algonkian Indians here. They lived much as we do, dwelling along a river and eating corn, beans, berries, and nuts. Though they are gone, Indian names remain: Mt. Wachusett and Mt. Monadnock and our own state's name, Massachusetts. A hundred years from now, when we are gone, maybe someone will play at Fruitlands as we play at Indians.

—⁓—

OCTOBER 10, 1843

We had one of our evenings of self-criticism. We do not shoot arrows as the Indians did, but we almost kill one another with words. I don't like having to criticize myself in front of every-one. It is like telling tales on yourself.

Here are this evening's self-criticisms. The interesting thing about them is that there is as much criticism of others as of oneself.

Father: I have not put pen to paper as often as I would wish. This is a great sorrow to me. If some of the others might take on more of my work, I would have time to bestow upon the world more of my valuable thoughts.

Mr. Lane: I regret that I have allowed myself to agree to the use of maple sugar. Mrs. Alcott has made the applesauce so sweet, it is impossible to savor the natural flavor of the apples.

Lizzie: I was so busy dressing my dolls I forgot to set the table tonight, and no one thought to remind me.

Mr. Bower: I regret that I have betrayed my principles by agreeing to the wearing of clothes, which confine the spirit as they confine the body. I do not see why others are so set in their prejudices as to require the constriction of shirts, trousers, and hats.

Anna: I was vain about the dirt from digging potatoes and wasted nearly a half hour in soaking my hands in soapy water and rubbing them with Mother's butternut oil. It does seem to me that the digging of potatoes ought to be done by the men, who need not care so much for their hands.

William: I did something wrong when I fed bread to a stray dog. It was only that the dog looked very hungry. It does seem that when Father chased the dog away, and scolded me for wasting food by giving it to an animal, he was forgetting that we must all be kind to animals.

Mother: I was too hard on everyone this morning, demanding that the house be weatherproofed. However, if I don't think of these things, no one else seems to. The girls are already complaining of the cold in the attic, and there are barely enough quilts and blankets to go around.

Me: We should have given over all of our time to the picking of the butternuts as we were told to do. Instead I tempted my sisters and William to lay our pails aside and play at Indians. We wasted an hour of time and caused the tear in my pantaloons and Lizzie's skinned knee. Also while we were playing, the squirrels got into our pails and we lost many of the nuts. William was very eager for the game.

Mr. Palmer: I should have finished cutting wood for the stove long since. I didn't stick to it and winter is close. My only excuse is that Bronson prefers the pen to the saw and the ax, leaving me to do his work for him. It is all very well to *write down a lot of ideas that look better on paper than they do in life, but if Bronson doesn't do his share, we are all bound to freeze.*

Mr. Palmer's words were very terrible. With his long beard and frown, I thought he looked like an Old Testament prophet. When he had finished there was a terrible silence. Father's face went white and then red. He dislikes being criticized. I think if he believed very strongly in himself, it wouldn't bother him so much. I hate to be criticized for something I already know is wrong. After a moment Father stamped out of the room leaving all of us (except for Mr. Palmer) feeling miserable. Mother went after Father to pacify him. If we keep shooting arrows at one another, no one will be left.

—ɯ—

OCTOBER 11, 1843

I have been very bad, and so have Anna and William. We are all sorry for what we did. Mother has taught us that fibs lead to lies, and lies tangle you into webs from which there is no escaping. So it was. Though we knew of it, Anna and I had told no one; William continued to play with the stray dog down near the river.

The poor dog was looking weak. William said he must have something more than bread. We had no flesh from animals for the dog, and no way to procure a piece of cow. William said he knew how to fish. I recalled seeing fishhooks at Fruitlands left by the last tenant. Anna said we must roast the fish, as the dog was not a seal or a walrus to eat the fish raw. I got the fishhooks. William caught the fish. Anna and I helped him roast it over a small fire while the dog looked on with his tongue hanging out.

Mr. Lane happened to be nearby and saw the smoke and discovered the fire and the fish before the dog had even one bite.

Mr. Lane and Father spoke very severely to us, telling us how the fish was one of God's creatures just as we were. I cried. Anna is in her room with a bad headache. William is up in the hayloft and won't come down. Mr. Palmer took the dog to a friend at a nearby farm.

—⁓—

OCTOBER 11, 1843

I felt badly for catching the fish, though I don't think the fish and I are so much alike in our feelings as Father says. I am sorry for William. Though Mother is kind to William, I believe he misses his own mother. The stray dog was not exactly a mother, but he was someone for William to love. Mr. Lane is a good man, but he is so upright in his behavior he would not be a father who could be easily loved.

I am sorry for Anna as well. Anna is so unhappy when Father is angry with her. When I am scolded I sulk and cry and stamp about having fits of remorse. In no time I have forgotten all about it. Anna says nothing when she is scolded but only cries and keeps all her misery inside herself. Then it turns into a headache that plagues her for the whole day.

—m—

OCTOBER 21, 1843

Is it possible? We have had snow. When I looked out of our attic window this morning, swatches of snow lay on the ground. The bare branches of the trees were frosted with white icing. Dabs of snow sat like little hats upon the tops of the pumpkins. The ugly heap of rubbish we have not yet buried has been bewitched into a sleeping polar bear. I shook Lizzie awake. We threw on our clothes and raced outside, Anna and William close behind. There was scarcely enough snow for a snowball fight but we did the best we could. By noon the sun had taken the snow away.

The men are chopping and splitting wood for winter fires. Mother said the chopping and splitting should have long since been done, but Father and Mr. Lane have been traveling to Boston and New York and even to Connecticut to seek new members for our family.

We were sent out to look for dead branches and twigs for kindling and to gather any squash left upon the ground. We put the squash in the cellar to keep. The carrots and parsnips will stay bravely in the chilly ground to sweeten.

After supper Mother knitted wool socks. There was some question about using wool, but Mother said no sheep dies from having its wool cut and sheep are probably happier in the summer with their heavy coats removed.

I and my sisters put on a play from Shakespeare.

OCTOBER 21, 1843

Mother wears a troubled look upon her face. I heard her say to Father that our barley and flour supplies are dwindling, and there is no money to buy more. This afternoon I walked into the kitchen without Mother hearing me and found her sitting with her hands over her face. I believe she had been crying. She quickly sent me off to fetch some apples. By the time I returned, she was busily at work shredding cabbage for our salad.

Yet Mother will say no word against Father's hopes. When Mr. Lane and Father are not nearby, Mr. Palmer grumbles, but Mother always takes Father's part. "Here at Fruitlands," she says, "we are pioneers in the improvement of mankind. No sacrifice is too great for such an undertaking."

This evening I heard a different story. I was helping her wash the dinner dishes. "Louy," she sighed, "sometimes I find myself wishing we were back in Concord in our little house with our dear friends around us." If Mother loses hope, how will I keep up my spirits?

To cheer Mother up we put on a play for her. She is fond of Shakespeare, so Anna, Lizzie, and I acted the three witches from Macbeth. We made pointed hats from paper and cloaks from bedspreads. We tangled our hair, put flour on our faces to make them white, and used a charred stick to darken the skin around our eyes. For a cauldron we borrowed the tub in which Mother boils her clothes. "Double, double toil and trouble," we chanted, "fire burn and cauldron bubble."

Anna: *Fillet of a fenny snake,*
                          In the cauldron boil and bake;
                          Eye of newt and toe of frog,
                          Wool of bat and tongue of dog,

Lizzie: *Adder's fork and blind-worm's sting,*
                          Lizard's leg and owlet's wing,
                          For a charm of powerful trouble,
                          Like a hell-broth boil and bubble.

Me: *Scale of dragon, tooth of wolf,*
                          Witches' mummy, maw and gulf
                          Of the ravin'd salt-sea shark,
                          Root of hemlock digged i' the dark . . .

As we tossed into the cauldron everything we could lay our hands on, from Father's nightcap to Mother's shoe and

Mr. Lane's toothbrush, there was much laughter. We stirred and stirred until at last I reached into the cauldron and pulled out Mother's corset.

Mother laughed so hard she could hardly get out the words, "That is surely the work of witches," for Mother hates her corset and will not wear it. When we went to bed we were all in a merry mood.

I awoke in the middle of the night to see if it had snowed again. It was too cold to go outside to the privy, so I used the chamber pot, though I will hate to empty it in the morning.

—⁓—

NOVEMBER 14, 1843

Anna and I have been sick, but not very sick. William is so ill he cannot even sit up in bed. He has been ill for two weeks. We tiptoe about the house and peek into his room to see how he is. Mother has made him barley water. There are no lessons. Mr. Lane spends all his time caring for William. Father is still traveling about looking for people to join us.

The winds have discovered every crack in the house. We wear our coats indoors as well as outdoors.

When I went to take the laundry from the line, it had frozen into stiff boards. It is amusing to see us talking in the house, for little clouds come out of our mouths just as though we were outdoors. We sit on our hands while we read and wear our caps to bed so that we look like elves. Anna creeps out of her room and up the stairway to the attic so we can all sleep close and cozy.

Though we packed the squash and turnips with straw when we put them in the cellar, they have frozen solid. We thaw them as we need them by putting them to bed with us for the night.

—⚮—

NOVEMBER 14, 1843

I do not see how things can get much worse. Our wood is running out, we have very little food, and there is no money to buy more. Father's spirits are low and Mother wears a frown. I know she has written to our uncle for money, but so far none has come. I heard her telling Father that we must leave Fruitlands while we are still all alive. Mother is so troubled, she has refused to sit down to meals with us. My sisters and

I are so upset at her absence, we can hardly eat.

Father will not listen. Only today he suggested taking apart the barn and carrying its wood into the forest far from human habitation. There he would build a house removed from all evil influences. I suppose we might as well freeze to death in the woods as at Fruitlands.

Mr. Bower has gone to live at Mr. Palmer's farm, so there is no one here but the Lanes, Mother and Father, and my sisters and me. Is it not sad that everyone has deserted us? I feel so sorry for Father and wonder what will come of his noble dreams for Fruitlands. If I thought staying all winter at Fruitlands would make Father's dream come true, I would gladly starve or freeze or even both. But I am afraid the starving or the freezing wouldn't help. Father's head is ever in the clouds. His noble thoughts keep him from feeling the cold wind or the hunger in his stomach. He does not see how cold and hungry we are.

Mr. Lane has surprised me very much. He has been caring for William day and night in a most tender way. He is such a stern man, not given to weakness, but he is ever so upset at William's illness. Yesterday he traveled through the snow to the farm where Mr. Palmer had taken the stray dog and brought it back to William. The dog sleeps on William's bed to keep William's toes warm and has all the bread it wants.

—✳—

November 29, 1843

Today we are all trying to be cheerful, for it is Father's birthday and my birthday as well. William is recovering and was able to join us for breakfast. Mother made corn cakes, which we had with maple syrup. Mr. Palmer came yesterday and brought a load of wood so that the room was nearly warm.

Mother gave Father socks she had knitted. Father received from Mr. Lane a book from Mr. Lane's library which Father has admired. William made a bookmark to go with the book. Abby May gave Father an abandoned bird's nest she had discovered in one of the alder bushes. After Father thanked her she insisted on taking it back, for she is very fond of it.

Anna, Lizzie, and I each wrote a poem for Father. He liked Anna's best, saying my poem, which was about snow falling on graves, was too unhappy a subject. When you are unhappy, I think it is more honest to write unhappy poems.

I received a new diary from Mother. Anna knitted mittens for me, and Lizzie mended the holes in my best stockings, something I kept forgetting to do. In the evening Father read some very pretty lines in Mr. Wordsworth's poem. My favorites lines in the poem are:

I wandered lonely as a cloud
That floats on high o'er vales and hills,
When all at once I saw a crowd,
A host, of golden daffodils . . .

Those words are so lovely they make me want to cry. I repeated the words "vales and hills" and "golden daffodils" over and over until Anna told me to stop. I wish I could write words that people would want to say over and over.

—∿—

NOVEMBER 29, 1843

Mother was once again at the dinner table, which was the best birthday present of all. She has told Father and Mr. Lane that she will not stay at Fruitlands. When she leaves, we are to go with her. I don't know whether I am glad or sorry. Certainly it is uncomfortable here in the cold with little food and daily sicknesses. Still, it is terrible to see Father's disappointment. He had such dreams for Fruitlands. He wanted Fruitlands to be a perfect place, but you cannot have a perfect place unless you have perfect people. And none of us has turned out to be perfect. I think I am the least perfect of all.

It's very sad to have to give up a dream. I don't think Father will be happy until he finds another dream. Mother and I are satisfied with the world as it is. Father wants to polish it until it shines like a diamond. I can't think that is wrong. I do think in a perfect world with perfect people, Father would be more considerate of Mother and would like me better.

Though Father is forty-four and I am only eleven, I cannot but feel that I am the older of the two, for I think more about wood for the fire and food for the table than Father does.

I went to sleep repeating to myself Mr. Wordsworth's lines.

—m—

Ours is a very sad house. We learned that when Mr. Lane went into Concord yesterday, he was put in jail for not paying taxes on Fruitlands. Mr. Palmer came to tell us. He had hurried so to bring us the terrible news that he had not taken the time to comb the crumbs from his beard. I saw that he had had more than plain bread to eat.

Mother and Father turned out their pockets to see if they could find enough money to release Mr. Lane. Mother had only pennies and Father had nothing at all. Mother said Father should travel to Concord to give Mr. Lane support and consolation. Father said the sight of Mr. Lane in prison would shrivel his soul and keep him from the work of finding new members for our family.

William was upset. I believe he thought he was to be an orphan. To cheer him up my sisters and I took him sledding down the hill with us. He was very sad at first, but after a few tumbles in the snow he cheered up.

A pale and shaken Mr. Lane arrived just before dark. A friend had paid the taxes. In the evening Father and Mother and Mr. Lane had a long talk.

—⚏—

December 2, 1843

Mother is always ready to help those in need, but who will help us? We have little food, and our firewood is nearly gone. Mr. Emerson no longer sends money. It is whispered that he told someone, "Alcott and Lane are always feeling of their shoulders to see if wings are sprouting." Mother wants us to leave Fruitlands, but Father says he will make another trip to New York to see if he can find support for his dream. Mr. Lane will go with him.

Mother said Father is like Christian in The Pilgrim's Progress, *who started out on his journey to the Celestial City without his wife and children. Father said Christian would gladly have taken his family on the journey, but they would not go. I am not sure I would wish to go on that journey, for Christian met with snares, traps, pits, blood, bones, hobgoblins, and dragons. It is bad enough to be cold and hungry.*

My sisters and I talked long into the night. Anna said, "We must do all we can to help Father's dream come true. I don't mind being a little hungry."

I said, "Mother is so unhappy, even if we don't mind being hungry, she minds that we are."

Lizzie said, "Even if this dream of Father's doesn't come true, he is sure to have another one."

—∿—

December 10, 1843

Mr. Lane and William are away. There is a blizzard outside so that we don't know when they will return. When you open the door, the snow blows into the house as if it were trying to move in. The springs are still flowing. Father says the water comes from a place so deep it cannot freeze. I wish I were in that place. The darkness comes by late afternoon.

I am writing a poem about a summer's day. I close my eyes and imagine a bright June afternoon with the sun dancing on the surface of the river. I imagine green and leafy trees and birds singing and the smell of lavender. I write it all down. After a while I hardly mind the cold.

This evening Father and Mother said they wished to have a serious talk with us. We all cried. I have resolved to be good and to give Mother and Father no trouble, for they have trouble enough.

—∭—

DECEMBER 10, 1843

This is the worst day we have ever had. It is not just that we are cold and hungry, but Mother says she is going to take my sisters and me and all the furniture and leave Fruitlands. The furniture belongs to her, for she brought it with her when she was married. Father refuses to leave. Mother pleaded with him, showing him how little food is left, only a few moldy turnips and some frozen squashes. There is too much snow to dig the carrots and parsnips, and mice have gotten into the barley.

"Full stomachs make for sluggish brains," Father said.

It was then that Mother said she would take the furniture. She has friends who are looking for a place for us to stay.

"Then you must go your way and I must go mine," Father said. We all cried, even Abby May, though I don't believe she knew what was happening. I begged Mother and Father not to part. I promised that I would mend my ways and be more cheerful and helpful. I sometimes feel everything is my fault. Though we talked for many hours, Father will not give up his dream and Mother will not see us starve. At last Mother promised that she would not leave until after Christmas.

Later when we were alone in the attic, Anna, Lizzie, and I talked and cried a lot. Anna said, "If Mother and Father separate, I'll stay with Father. He could never get along by himself."

"Anna," I pleaded, "what about Mother? We are everything to her. I could never leave her."

Lizzie said, "Father and Mother will never part. I am sure of it."

—⁂—

DECEMBER 25, 1843

Father has gone to Boston to a meeting, walking the entire thirty-five miles through the cold and snow. Mother, my sisters and I, William, and Mr. Lane celebrated Christmas as best we could. Outside, the snow fell without a sound, but what a difference it made. Swaths of snow hang over the tops of the windows, and snow piles up on the ground so that nothing is familiar. Mr. Lane cut a small pine tree, and Anna and I decorated the mantel with pine boughs. Pine fragrance fills the whole room so that it is like living in a forest.

Lizzie cut paper dolls and hung them on the tree. I

helped Abby May string the dried cranberries we picked this summer in a nearby bog. Mr. Lane is generous with the wood, so that the room is warm and bright. Our gifts were pincushions, pen wipers, scarfs, socks we knitted, and poems and stories we wrote for one another.

Later Mr. Palmer and the Lovejoys drove over on the Lovejoys' sleigh. The Lovejoys are neighbors of Mr. Palmer. They brought a Christmas pudding, which we all ate, even Mr. Lane, though I fear it was full of forbidden things. Mr. Lane brought out his violin and we sang the ballads of Thomas Moore and our favorite carols. It would have been a merry Christmas if only Father had been here.

—⁓—

DECEMBER 25, 1843

William told us a secret. Mr. Lane has been visiting the Shakers. He is planning on leaving Fruitlands to join them. William does not want to go but thinks he will have to. Though he cannot bring himself to say so, I believe he will miss us. I told him that there were friendly people at the Shakers' and a warm bathtub besides. He only sighed a great sigh.

It will just about kill Father if Mr. Lane leaves Fruitlands. In truth, I shall be sorry to see him go. Since William was so ill, Mr. Lane has been more mild, not even scolding us when we come unprepared for lessons. Today he said nothing when Mother used a great deal of wood to warm the room. Nor was anything said when the table was heaped with the last of the barley and nearly all of our apples. While we are finally warm and our stomachs are full, I believe such generosity can only mean we will soon leave Fruitlands.

In spite of all of our worries we sang loudly and with much spirit. We had a game of blindman's buff which even Mr. Lane joined. We all laughed when with his blindfold on he could not tell the difference between Anna and me until he felt Anna's curls. William looked rather sad, and I know he was thinking there would be no games of blindman's buff at the Shakers'.

Before the Lovejoys left they took Mother aside, and I heard her accept their kind offer of three rooms. I told Anna and Lizzie what I heard. We are afraid to ask Mother if Father will live with us in those three rooms.

When I looked out of the attic window I saw that the snow had ended. The moon was shining, striping the snow with black tree shadows. An owl settled down on the granary roof. I believe it was looking for some small creature to pounce on. I felt sorry for that small creature. I felt sorry for Father all alone on Christmas.

—⚏—

JANUARY 6, 1844

Father has returned, only to have to say farewell to Mr. Lane and William, who left today. We all embraced William and wished him well, promising to come to see him. We shook Mr. Lane's hand and thanked him for helping us with our lessons. After they left, Father went to his room and has not come out, not for dinner or for supper. Mother took a tray with food to him, but when we went to say good night, the food was still on the tray.

—⚏—

JANUARY 6, 1844

I never did see such misery. Father sat in a chair watching as William and Mr. Lane carried out their books and loaded them onto Mr. Palmer's wagon. I don't know who was the more upset, Father watching or Mr. Lane being watched.

Mother and I and all of my sisters cried when the Lanes left. Abby May hung on to William and did not want to let him go. When at last they were gone, Father went into his bedroom and lay upon the bed. He turned his face to the wall.

When Mother begged him to take some food, he repeated Christian's words from The Pilgrim's Progress, "I see myself now at the end of my journey; my toilsome days are ended."

What can Father mean? Mother has been crying.

Now that William is gone Lizzie and I have a room of our own. We put up some pretty pictures, and Mother gave us a dresser scarf with real lace. Lizzie's dolls sit on her bed. My journal (the public one) lies open on our desk next to the pens and ink. The room looks very nice, but I would gladly give it up to have William back.

—m—

JANUARY 9, 1844

Father has had nothing to eat for three days. He lies in bed, pale and weak. Mother keeps food by his bed but he does not touch it. He lies there staring at the ceiling. Mother pleads with him. She says he is starving himself. Mother read aloud to him the part from *The Pilgrim's Progress* that says "For one to kill himself is to kill body and soul at once."

Father did not listen, but only turned his back. He whispered that all of his dreams have come to nothing and there is no reason for him to continue on the Earth. He spoke only of his failures. Words of encouragement have come from Mr. Emerson, but Father will not hear them.

Anna and I crept up to Father's bed. Anna told him all that he has accomplished, reminding him of the schools where he taught and how his kindness and his respectful treatment of students have made him famous all over the world. His teachings have changed the way children are taught in schools.

I pleaded as well, but it was Lizzie's question that reached him. "You won't leave us all alone, Father?" she pleaded.

He gave a great sigh. "No, Lizzie, I won't. Even in my worst days your mother and you and your sisters have have not deserted me. I must not desert you."

Mother walked into the room. When she heard

Father speak, she gave him a bit of bread and barley water, which he ate and drank. He closed his eyes and we tiptoed out. An hour later, when we returned, Father was sitting up in bed and making plans.

"I must write the history of Fruitlands," he said. "We cannot allow the lessons of this grand experiment to be lost. We were so close to our goal and it was such a noble one." When Father asked for pen and ink, I knew all was well.

—⁓—

JANUARY 9, 1844

We are all to leave Fruitlands in two days' time for the Lovejoys' house. I wonder if I could have done more to help Father's dream come true. Perhaps so. It was hard to see Father so sad. Is it possible that he expected too much and was bound to be disappointed? Still, who else can boast of so strange and wonderful a year. I would not change it for anything.

From the window of my room I can look out at the woods where we celebrated Lizzie's birthday. The river where we had our shower baths is nearly iced over. The hills I ran over are white humps. In the orchard the tops of the new trees stick

bravely out of the snow. I cannot think Fruitlands will be
happy without us.

—〰—

JANUARY 11, 1844

My sisters and I gathered together all of our things.
They fill only one box. The last of the wood burns in
the fireplace. Mother is packing what food is left and
Father is filling a box with his letters and papers.

In the afternoon Mr. Lovejoy will come for us. We
have no money to pay them, but Father, who is a clever
carpenter, will turn his hand to building and repairing
in exchange for room and board. Mother will help out
with her sewing and embroidery.

Fruitlands' empty rooms seem haunted by all those
who lived here this year. Lazy Miss Page, Mr. Bower
sulking in his room, Abraham wringing out the clothes
for Mother, and William, who became our friend.
Everywhere we look I see the ghost of Mr. Lane, who
shared Father's dream but none of Father's joy in it.

—〰—

JANUARY 11, 1844

When I asked Mother if Father's dream for Fruitlands was a failure, Mother said it was not. With a gentle smile she said, "Think how much our efforts have taught us about ourselves this year. The failure, if failure it was, is only in how your father's dream of a happy, useful community was carried out. The failure was not in your father's dream."

That made me feel better, but I resolved that after this I will have my own dreams.

AFTERWORD

This is what happened to everyone after they left Fruitlands:

Wood Abram *published a book entitled* My First and Last Book.

Samuel Bower *stayed with Mr. Palmer, but longed to travel to a warmer climate where clothes would be less necessary.*

Abraham Everett *worked at his cooper's trade.*

Isaac Thomas Hecker *became a Roman Catholic priest and founded the Paulist Fathers.*

Mr. Lane and William *returned to England, where Mr. Lane opened a school.*

Samuel Larnard *returned to Providence.*

Ann Page *was active in the women's suffrage movement.*

Joseph Palmer *purchased Fruitlands from Mr. Lane. For twenty years anyone in need found a welcome and food and shelter there.*

Louisa and her family *had many more adventures, but in our hearts we will think of them forever as we know them in* Little Women.

BIBLIOGRAPHY

Alcott, Louisa M. *Louisa May Alcott: Her Life, Letters, and Journals*. Boston: Roberts Brothers, 1889.

Bedell, Madelon. *The Alcotts: Biography of a Family*. New York: Clarkson N. Potter, 1980.

John Bunyan. *The Pilgrim's Progress*. Uhrichville, Ohio: Barbour Publishing, 1993.

O'Brien, Harriet E. *Lost Utopias: A Brief Description of Three Quests for Happiness*. Brookline, Mass., 1947.

Saxton, Martha. *Louisa May: A Modern Biography of Louisa May Alcott*. Boston: Houghton Mifflin, 1977.

Sears, Clara Endicott, ed. *Bronson Alcott's Fruitlands*. Philadelphia: Porcupine Press, 1975.

Willis, F.L.H. [Frederick Llewellyn Hovey]. *Alcott Memoirs*. Boston: R. G. Badger, 1915.

GLORIA WHELAN

is a distinguished poet and award-winning author. She
has written many books for young readers, including
Homeless Bird, winner of the National Book Award;
Angel on the Square; *Return to the Island*; *Once on this
Island*, winner of the Great Lakes Book Award; *Farewell
to the Island*; *Miranda's Last Stand*; and *The Indian School*.
Ms. Whelan lives with her husband, Joseph, in the
woods of northern Michigan.